Luna Station Quarterly

Issue 028 | December 2016

Editor & Publisher

Jennifer Lyn Parsons

Assistant Editors

Tara Calaby
Cathrin Hagey
Andi Marquette
Dana Mele
Megan Patton
Danielle Perry
Iona Sharma

Cover Artist

Sara Kipin

LUNA STATION PRESS

Luna Station Quarterly publishes short fiction on March 1st, June 1st,
September 1st, and December 1st. For more information and submission
guidelines, please visit our website at lunastationquarterly.com

For Luna Station Press

Creative Director - Tara Quinn Lindsey

LUNA STATION PRESS

576 Valley Road #197
Wayne, NJ 07470

www.lunastationpress.com

info@lunastationpress.com

CONTENTS

EDITORIAL

Jennifer Lyn Parsons

By the time you read this, the election will have been over for almost a month. I have no concept, sitting here on November 19th, of what that might feel like. I still don't really have the words I need to write this editorial, but here I am anyway. Because that's what I need to do right now. I need to be here, feeling whatever I'm feeling, right alongside you.

And I'm feeling a lot of things.

Fear. Sadness. Shock. Anger. Disappointment. All of those and more, sometimes simultaneously and all of them cycling from day to day, moment to moment.

I finally sat down and pulled my thoughts together, even if they're not so very cohesive. The narrative thread never presented itself, but I feel like that's reflective of where we are right now, when so much feels vertiginous.

So, here are a few things I have been thinking about.

I finally sat down to the Hamilton soundtrack for the first time a few days ago. I think something told me to save it until i really needed it. Growing up on the East Coast of the U.S., my family took me to all the Revolutionary War stuff. New Jersey has a bunch of historical sites on its own, plus we went to Boston a couple times, down to Colonial Williamsburg a lot, etc. That whole period of our history means a lot to me on a core level and I'm reconnecting with all that now. It's pretty powerful.

Part of the reason I'm so drawn to that period now is that I can look back on those people who founded this country and use them as touchstones. Not just wondering what they would have thought of the state of politics, but who we have become as a people. Lest we forget, the founding fathers were a bunch of radicals. They pushed buttons. They were obnoxious and disliked. They were a bunch of immigrants changing the very shape of the world so that people could live free lives.

They stayed and they fought.

One question I've been asking myself over the last week or so is where does that leave Luna Station Quarterly? Where do we go from here? I don't know what 2017 and beyond will look like for the world, but for LSQ there are a couple of things I do know.

First, we're not going anywhere. Stories are more important now than ever. They provide comfort, hope, and perspective, as well as the necessary escapism (which has never been an ugly word to me) needed to keep our batteries charged. Top to bottom, our staff is passionate about keeping that mission moving forward.

Secondly, LSQ has always been about inclusivity. In the past, this has been mostly focused on women as a marginalized group, but that's changing for us. While our mission remains focused on women, what it means to be a woman (or more accurately, "not a man") is open to a lot more interpretation than it was even just a few years ago.

Racially and ethnically, we want to see more diverse voices in our pages as well. While I do not feel we have failed in this area, it's something I know we can do better on. I hope you all will help us get there.

I am listening.

A lot of us are searching for where to put our energy now. Do we protest, do we apply diplomacy across the aisle, do we batten down the hatches and hide? I cannot tell any of you what is best for you, what you need to do.

For myself? I have a job to do. First and foremost, I am a caretaker. I will make sure everyone is drinking enough water, that everyone has eaten, that everyone gets some rest. LSQ is part of that job. In sending stories out into the world, we're providing a respite and a refuge.

Our stories give us strength.

When I look at LSQ I feel a sense of pride for what we are and who we represent. The world has changed and will continue changing, but we have not come this far to let everything we have fought for go so easily.

It will be hard, yes. There may be backsliding before we move forward again, and we have no way of knowing right now how far we'll go. But we have each other. We are not alone. The internet has connected us all and given us undeniable proof that no matter who you are or what you are feeling, you are not alone.

And so we gather around tables and feed each other and talk and cry together. We plan and organize and make a safe spaces for those who need to feel safe. We keep making art and telling stories because right now, the world needs more art and more stories.

There is hope in stories.

Those are my thoughts for you. I'll see you in the next issue. Until then, stay safe.

LSQ|028

CARA'S HEARTSONG

Dawn Bonanno

Dawn Bonanno suffers from an obsession with pens, paper and fixing things, so it only makes sense that she writes stories. She blogs about her writing journey at www.dmbonanno.com.

After the bombs rained like fire and the riots faded, my daughter and I found ourselves alone in her room, our home surrounded by silence so deep it gouged my soul. The grandfather clock downstairs chimed once an hour, and rattled too, the cracked glass panel vibrating with the chimes. In the silence between chimes, Cara's heart beat too quietly, too slow, and out of sync.

Cara squeezed my arm, her breath labored and her face pale, like the ghost she was in danger of becoming. "Mama, am I dying?"

My heart hitched on a breath and for an endless moment I couldn't speak. "Yes, my love. Your heartsong is still fading."

Before the attack, the answer would have been different, but three long days had passed without power, water, or contact. No National Guard, no Red Cross. How many homes had fallen across the city, the state, the country? How many husbands never made it home? How many children died waiting for life-saving surgeries?

Cara shifted onto her side. She cuddled Snickerpoodle, the relic of a windup doll my mom gave her last Christmas before she herself succumbed to illness. I rubbed Snickerpoodle's curly black hair, earning a weak smile from my daughter.

"Can you fix my heart?"

Just days ago, I'd fought for that very thing, but hospital rules prohibited me operating on family. The rules had changed, but without power or medical staff, how could I save Cara? "I'll think of something," I said and smiled, because her confidence in me was all she had left.

I snuggled her until the grandfather clock chimed again. The damned clock was the only sound, the only evidence we had survived. What made it special, a stupid invention of wood, gears and glass? I bolted upright. Gears.

I slipped out of Cara's bed and ran around the house, tossing supplies into Cara's backpack, then returned and lifted her too-light body in my arms.

Our two-family home stood undamaged, the only one on this street now, but my Rav4 sat in the driveway surrounded by debris and a dangling gas cap. No matter, I had two feet. I hugged Cara to my chest; she wrapped her legs around my waist, rested her head on my shoulder, and we began the long walk to the hospital.

The sidewalks were damp with drying rain, puddles attracted to the cracks. The fires must have died during last night's rain, but the stench of smoldering rubber and flesh irritated my nostrils. I nudged Cara's face against my neck to protect her from it. Glass and debris carpeted the street right up to the hospital, blood spattered generously.

Whenever we passed a body, I averted my gaze. There was no one to help here, and no hope of finding my beloved David. If he hadn't returned home after the riots, he never would.

I stepped through the busted hospital doors, breathless after the long hike. Sunlight streamed in through window frames, creating pockets of glimmering light across the shadowed corridors. It got us to the main stairway and up to the O.R., which was windowless and dark. I felt my way around and lay Cara on a gurney, then raided the emergency supplies for a flashlight.

The stench in the room was worse for regaining my vision. Someone had abandoned a surgery, left their patient, her surgical meds.

Whispering a prayer for the dead woman, I thanked her for sharing her medication. I loaded the gurney with surgical tools and bandages, everything my imaginary nurse would hand me during Cara's surgery. I kept my backpack close, the metal contents clinking together now and again. It sounded like hope. Or perhaps insanity.

After a quick search of the second floor, a corner office aglow with the late morning sun became my operating room. I scrubbed with bottled water and alcohol until my fingers burned, then washed and laid out all my tools: meds, needle, thread, surgical knives, gears harvested from the grandfather clock and more. My gaze fell on the gears, too large to fit into my daughter's chest cavity now that I can compare them. Tears stung my eyes. I'd come too far to give up on Cara, too far to admit defeat.

Cara followed my movements, hugging Snickerpoodle, a doll that has lasted the last hundred years through generations of my family, a doll that was about to outlive us. "What are we doing, Mama?"

"Fixing your heart, love."

"Then we'll go find Daddy?"

Now was not the time for the truth. "Soon as you're up for it."

I leaned close, stroked the doll's brown face. We'd repainted the eyes twice since Cara acquired it, once to give her sight and the second to have the eyes match Cara's brown.

How had such a thing survived? My lips went suddenly dry,

my breath stolen from my lungs. "Cara, I have to ask a favor. It's important."

She nodded, the barest of movements.

"Would Snickerpoodle like to donate some organs?"

"Will I get her back?"

"Yes, but she'll be a little different."

Cara bit her lip, considering, then smiled. "I'll still love her."

"She's a brave little girl." After kissing Cara's forehead, I started an IV with a small dose of the sedative. Waiting for it to take effect, I washed her chest with alcohol, swirling little dances with my fingers, tickling, sending my sweetheart off to dreamland with a smile.

The sunlight pushed through the room and faded with the afternoon as I sliced my daughter's chest open. Her little heart was warm to the touch. Its song pulsated against my fingers as softly as any heart I'd ever touched. My life's work was in the operating room, fixing little hearts, and I'd heard so many over the years, each with its own cadence and tone. Nothing tore me down faster than this song, which I've heard before, in the chests of little ones I couldn't save.

My own heart drummed too quickly, but my hands were steady, and the augmentation eased into place. Closing and stitching went smoothly. I waited until dusk, pacing, watching her chest rise and fall until I couldn't keep my eyes open.

I melted to the floor and curled into dreamless sleep, waking only when Cara whimpered.

"Mama?"

"I'm here." I sprang up, panicked, and gripped her bedrail for balance.

Cara squinted and looked around. "Where's Snickerpoodle?"

"Here," I pressed the doll into her hands.

"And her winder-upper?"

I took Cara's hand and put it to her left side, next to her heart. The metal was warm between our fingers, warmer than her heart had been last night. I'd have to teach her to wind and clean the key, but we had time for that. Maybe not forever, but today and as many stolen moments as my clockwork daughter could rally, if only she accepted the changes, and if the magic worked. Magic lived in the doll; had protected my ancestors right up until my mom gave it to Cara. Nothing else could explain the unlikely events leading to our survival.

She listened. "Mommy, what happened to my heartbeat?"

"Snickerpoodle isn't the only one who's a little different now," I said softly. "Tell me, love, how does it feel?"

"My heart hums, like Snickerpoodle used to."

"Is it humming a good song?"

Cara caressed the empty key socket then explored her side again. Her cheeks were flush for the first time in a year. She took a deep long breath. "You made me a new heartsong, Mommy, and it's good."

THE QUESTION OF THE BLADE

Alex Yuschik

Alex Yuschik is a graduate student in Mathematics at the University of Pittsburgh. She likes obscure alphabets, fast cars, and watching the sun rise over cities.

She was nine when she became a Knife.

Onyx pebbles pressed into her feet as she ran with the opposing team's flag streaming out behind her, a crown of dried orange lantern flowers clattering against her head like rain. Two years had passed since she washed ashore on this island where no one could say her name properly, two years since she became Fel Valens instead of the girl she was.

Wisteria-crowned playfellows streaked after her, but Fel was faster than all of them and she didn't stop until she crashed into Bas and knocked them both to the dirt, a mess of limbs and sweat and victory whoops.

"I knew you'd win," Bas said, her own lantern-flowers knocking Fel's askew. When Bas was captain, no one had to ask who she'd pick first. It never changed.

Fel shrugged like it was nothing and handed her the flag.

They were always on each other's team, sneaking into the novices' rooms to steal peeks at the day's horoscopes, inspecting the bottomsides of fallen cherry leaves for calligraphy. Sometimes they'd find one with their names written on it in telltale white ink, and Bas would charm the kitchen staff into giving them honeycakes while Fel glowered at the other kids who so much as thought to tattle until they ran away. The pair would pour over the leaf, Bas trying to figure it out and Fel pretending equally hard that she knew how.

But the fortunes always said the same thing.

That day after the game, they were walking back to ply Bas' chefs for victory snacks when her governess steered her inside and tched at her dirt-scribbled face. Fel stood at the shut door for some time, lantern flower pods still perched on her head, waiting. She was rude, adults told her, because she didn't know better.

Eventually, the governess sighed and opened the door. "The Lei line has always sent their descendants to the scriptorium," she said.

It took a while to go through the whole story and Fel didn't understand most of it. The governess was by then sweating in the early summer heat, so she settled on: "Bas is busy."

"When will she not be busy?" Fel asked. Bas kept their entire shared collection of pumice stones in her room and Fel had wanted to add more specimens today.

"If she's as peony-blooded as we think, probably never." The governess leaned against the doorjamb as Fel resolutely did not pick up on the hint. "Are there any flowers in your blood?"

Fel was fairly sure there weren't. She knew it the same way she knew she was rude, not because she sensed something lacking but because what she had never seemed to amaze people. Whenever she got cut all that came out was red.

A plume of ash-gray smoke rose from the palace's latest pyre, and the governess sighed again and shooed Fel out into the lane. "If Lei Basalt's smart, she'll choose a Sword that can keep her alive longer than a damn year."

"A Sword?"

The governess pulled a familiar leaf from her pocket and studied the tilt of the tines, still visible even after Fel and Bas had crumpled it in their studies. The governess scowled at Fel, but not like it was her fault. "The Weapons office is by the carpenter's. Run, and you should make it before they close."

She shut the door, hard this time. Fel ran.

***

Twelve. It was a fine age for promotion, even if the hardest ceremonial she could execute without difficulty was the Form of the Fish. The abbreviated Form of the Hexagon (with points) still made the new muscles on her shoulders ache.

But it turned out that assailants did not particularly care whether or not you could do the Form of the Fish or even the Form of the Hexagon, with or without the points—all that mattered was whether you could kill them before they killed you or the person you were assigned to protect. Fel had won.

And so she passed from Knife to Dagger.

"I hate this," Bas said, throwing another stick into the bone-white char of the pyre. They wore carnelian again, because the High Enchanter was dead and that made it an obligatory festival day. Fel never understood why it was a festival when people you liked died, but that, the initiates said, only proved she was more at home in the Profane than in the Sacred.

"You are supposed to be holy right now." She tipped her chin at Bas' sleeves as the other girl pouted near the embers. "Watch out, you're crisping something."

Assailant. That was the word they used in Knife training, and she'd thought it meant human.

Loftily, Bas shook the ash out of her ritual garb and made a gesture that was not befitting of her station.

"Go on, do the thing already." Fel began another walk along the perimeter. She did not like remembering the mutual shudder, let alone how much of the assailant's mortal wound had been an accident.

"Fine, but I'm using your coordinates," Bas called, waving the leaf and a charcoal stick. "Hey, come back. Don't you want to know it what it says?"

Fel's personal horoscope that day had been something innocuous like *small luck*, or *possibility of minor accident ahead*, not *you will kill a living thing*. *We trade in fortunes*, she'd spat at Bas. *Those things are trying to kill you for this and it's not even useful*. But Bas said that was how just how it worked: because no one knew the precise moment of Fel's birth—though she did know the date and that it had been in the morning—the details were, necessarily, vague.

"I already know." Fel had heard it enough. "'Fel Valens will be as a blade to Lei Basalt.'"

Bas threw a handful of leaves into the air and twirled her charcoal as they fell, reciting the rest. "'But whether Lei Basalt commands her or stands before her as an enemy is up to question.'"

"It is not," Fel said and swept off on another circuit.

Behind them, high-ranked enchanters scried on bark backs and fern-stem wafers, burning incense to disguise the lingering scent of peonies.

Some people had flowers in their blood. And some things wanted to cut the flowers out.

All the acolytes took turns watching the pyre, and all things told it was a smoothly run affair. Perhaps because the Sacreds disliked more upset than necessary in these transitions. Or perhaps it was because this always happened in the late spring or early summer when the egg-shaped buds of peonies became too full. Voices traipsed through winding staircases of hymns, and Bas replaced the leaves warding the late High Enchanter's body whenever the writing on them got sooty.

The wards themselves were string ladders of tiny offerings tied around the funeral pyre, spare lines written on the back of plum and cherry leaves. Bas' ink strokes were, of course, easiest to recognize: her letters snow fish frozen mid-swim, ink glistening on sickled bones.

Fel's new captain had told her that making Dagger this young was a reward, along with getting to guard the most talented of the acolytes as she mended the pyre's barriers. Mostly, she felt tired. Mostly, she felt like she'd learned something too fast to understand it.

But for that moment, watching Bas' face light up when her words glowed without any help from the fire, it mostly felt worth it.

***

Three years of being a Dagger and she'd stopped worrying about being rude. It was what she was supposed to do, and enchanters' sneers sluiced off her like water off a duck. Like these hellish adept's silks kept doing.

She grimaced when Bas adjusted them for the sixth time, and when Fel hunched her shoulders the gentle fabric pulled taut. "Can't do a damn form in these."

"Why would I need to?" Bas squinted at the intricate confection she'd made from Fel's unruly hair and then threaded in another opalite hair stick with a pained expression. "Well, you almost pass."

"Almost isn't good enough," Fel said. Almost didn't protect the High Enchanter. Almost didn't kill on first strike. That's the first conduct of the profane, to protect the sacred. And there was nothing in this room more profane than she was and nothing more sacred than Bas. "Those things are made of mirrors. It's got to be perfect or they'll know I'm not you."

Bas fluffed Fel's hair again with the air of someone attempting a particularly challenging puzzle. "They'll figure it out sooner or later. Then what?"

Then they'll tell the Mirror Queen, Fel didn't say.

And that was the thing. She was only a Dagger, but it was impossible not to know the score. The Mirror Queen only tolerated enchanters so long before she sent her sharp subjects through portals to get rid of them, and a Blade worthy of her title would die before the High Enchanter whose weapon she was. A poor Sword meant another summer pyre and pale smoke, incense and hazy casting for fresh, fortune-favored blood.

Bas knew it too, but she stuck her tongue out. "Try smiling more, Val."

Fel did, and both of them agreed it was perhaps best that she pretend to be a surly version of Lei Basalt for the evening.

Even before Bas had gotten too good to be ignored, the Sacreds were already whispering about the Lei line and its latest scion. After Bas earned her adept's robes, Fel had taken her out to lie on their backs in the wet grass, to catch the last rain falling through the branches and pick out the shapes of imaginary monsters that the gaps in tree leaves created.

These days there was more than one kind of negative space around Bas.

And Fel had sworn to fill it.

"Just stay hidden. No matter what." Fel tucked the robe into her sash unevenly, and Bas tucked herself into the secret compartment under the floors and didn't come out, not even when the mirror creatures stormed the adepts' quarters and Fel's twin daggers shattered them one after another into fragments and dust. If none escaped, none could report back to the Mirror Queen. Simple enough.

It was only when Fel knocked twice on the floorboard door, steps shuffling, blades hanging limply by her sides, that Bas popped her head up. To her left, the opalite hairstick protruded from the eyesocket of a dead mirror monster, and the whole room was littered with broken glass. "All gone?"

"This robe," Fel said, "is so stupid."

Then she collapsed in a heap of blood-stained, shredded silks.

Fel Valens didn't have a drop of peony blood in her. But from the way that Bas called for towels, for fresh-picked leaves with straight spines and her best calligraphy pens, yelled for her novices to bring all these as fast as possible, you'd never know it.

***

It wasn't until she was sixteen that the inevitable finally happened.

"I need to take the test," Fel said, out of breath, to the Captain of Swords. She'd been in training when she heard the news and she was still sweaty, heart stuttering.

"Look, Dagger. I know you've long been friends with the Enchanter Elect. I also know what the horoscopes say." The Captain huffed. She'd looked favorably on Fel's spirited defense of Bas a year prior, and Fel's dagger work, devotion to daily ceremonials, and impressive kill count over the past few months hadn't hurt the Captain's opinion of her. "Good Swords are hard enough to find these days without my breaking the blade prematurely. Give it a year."

A year was too late. The ceremony was tonight, and there would be no fooling the Mirror Queen anymore.

The Captain ran a hand through her close-cropped hair. "Remember the last Dagger who tested early? A week's recovery he needed. Then he quit. You'll just get an ass-whooping."

Fel unsheathed her daggers. "With all due respect, Captain."

Begrudgingly, the Captain raised her sword. "Then make it good. Swordsmanship isn't only about wanting it badly enough."

"I know," Fel said and schooled her breathing into a familiar Form. "But wanting it's no small part."

Three hours later, after she'd put on her new armor and marched into the High Enchanter's hall, everything still hurt.

Bas' initiation took place in the ashes once the pyre had burnt itself out and, by the time Fel arrived, was nearly over.

Passing in two hours would have allowed her to witness the ritual start to finish, from the procession to the lettering. She was late because the Captain of Swords had made her late, would not let her go until she'd tested every move, but Fel had not missed this essential part.

"High Enchanter," the Captain said, herself still out of breath, to Bas. "Choose your Sword."

Bas' face was made up in dark swipes of cursive kohl, patterned silks trailing after her in strokes of ink. She was trying to hide it, but Fel knew the tells: hands folding and unfolding themselves like fresh laundry, eyes downcast or lingering on the ceiling but never stopping in the middle distance.

Fel was pushed into the ranks of Swords by an attendant and she stood at parade rest, back religiously straight even as her aching legs fought for balance. Fronds crisped, smoke rose, and peonies trapped in vases shuddered open. She was cultivating a black eye and hadn't had time to clean up all the blood, but Bas found her anyway.

Because all fortunes said the same thing when it came to Fel Valens and Lei Basalt.

"And may she be a Blade to defend you against all ills, all evils, and all dangers."

A smile bloomed on the new High Enchanter's face and for a second Fel could swear flowers moved through her too, petals under her skin flooding from head to heart to hand to throat. Bas held the weapon hilt-end out, wrapped in glittering cloth. "Fel Valens, my Blade."

Fel accepted it and knelt, the ritual words repeating in elliptic loops of sleepsong in her head, and it was done and done and done.

* * *

But all flowers fade.

Mirror creatures crawled out of bronze plates and calm lakes—any surface level enough to cast a reflection. Fel stalked them through corridors and storerooms, underground and across courtyards until she crunched their mirror sides to gravel. Let that be a message to their Queen. Her boots clacked over the roof and its bright tiles after rain, cutting down shimmering legions as they rose like spectres in the mist.

She was the Blade of the High Enchanter, and all through that summer, fall, and winter when she moved her clothes and armor scattered diamond dust.

And there was praise, from her Captain, from the other Swords, who hated her and her smug, glowering face until they found their jobs easier. From the people, when their High Enchanter threw a gala celebrating her first year in residence after the dangerous season of peony blossoms had passed, that summer night warm and full of firecrackers and sweets wrapped in plum leaves.

There were medals and commendations, specially commissioned plates for her armor, but most of all there were ribbons from Bas. Little things, scraps to wear around a wrist or tuck into a pocket, things that weren't meant to be seen.

Fel knew they were there and so did Bas, and that was all that mattered.

Perhaps it was not surprising that she became what she became, something not meant to be seen, the shadow that waited for rain or clouded mirrors. And perhaps they should have seen it when her body count rose and village jewelers scrambled to find uses for the excess glass and gilt, when diamond blades made their way into every seahouse's kitchen and children pared fruit with them at lunch, lost them to no consequence.

The clean-up crew might have said something, its duties increasing each morning when Fel went to bed. But if they wanted to mention it to the High Enchanter as she was selecting her ink wells and choosing the smoothest leaves for the day's horoscopes, her breakfast honeycakes in a pyramid on the dish at her side as her Blade slept in her still-warm sheets, perhaps they remembered the pyres and how nice this new kind of permanence had been.

This High Enchanter tracked them along a propitious future written out in neat, assured italic, and a little more work on their part was no reason to disrupt a course they'd strived so long to tread.

And so Fel Valens stained the roof black with mirror blood, retreating only in the small hours of the morning, when the moon was no longer capable of rallying ghosts, when the night around her was too absolute to cast a shadow.

They hated to say it, but all was well.

***

"Please forgive me."

Fel didn't hear her the first time. When Fel passed Bas' advisors on the way to her summons, they snickered in the corridors. When she glowered at them with dark blood and mirrorglass stuck to her armor in corrupted spikes, they glowered back, saying things like *up to question* and *remains unclear*.

But that was nothing. It had been her and Bas at the beginning and it would be her and Bas at the end. That was what every horoscope about them meant, and all four years into Bas' reign they'd been right.

Sometimes Bas took her aside to tell her that she didn't have to kill all the mirror creatures that came through. Sometimes

Fel reminded Bas that she was the longest-lived High Enchanter for a reason and that power had to be exercised to be felt.

"You asked for me, Sacred?" Blood snaked down Fel's arm, only some of it hers.

"Sword." Bas nodded, just like normal.

So when Bas told her to kneel and placed the same lantern flower crown on Fel's head from years ago, Fel was amused but knelt all the same. She was a blade wielded and she did not regret it, whatever the advisors said.

The magic didn't take effect until she stood.

"What the hell is this, Bas?" Fel gritted, arms frozen halfway up to rip the crown from her head, unable to move them farther. Her feet were rooted to the tiles.

"It's wholesale slaughter. You never listen when I tell you to stop," Bas said, eyes shining. "All I wanted was to live, not be a queen of corpses."

"They're enemies." Fel shook with effort as the bonds forced her to all fours, but moved one hand from the ground to the pommel of her sword, then to the grip.

"They used to be. Now no one's seen them around for months. One night, I stayed up and watched you. You hunt them out before they even attack. They run back to the mirrors because they're scared and you don't stop. You pull them back and cut them open. They bow and plead and surrender and you still don't stop."

"If I stop, you die," Fel hissed. "Did your useless advisors tell you that before they told you to do this?"

Fel Valens was the one question no horoscope could answer. She should have seen this coming.

But she hadn't, and now the seal on the floor flared to life and fear prickled through her. "What are you doing?"

"Fixing this. There's got to be a way we can make peace with the Mirror Queen. Find it. Please forgive me, Val." Bas swiped a tear from her face and held a calligraphed leaf between two fingers, shaking. "I won't let you become a monster."

The floor below Fel shifted. All at once she was standing on a giant mirror and she knew what was going to happen. She struggled and spat at Bas' feet. "I already am."

"This wasn't what I wanted," Bas blinked, fast, but held the leaf steady, "when I asked you to be my Blade."

"Bas," Fel said as the letters took hold and the ground rippled, "Bas, wait—"

But then there was nothing but silence.

***

For a while, the world was full of sharp darkness and edges that gleamed. There was cut-sweep-dodge-stagger-blood. There was a sword, thank all the gods and every shadow. There were many kinds of nothingness, and after a time the person with the sword got good at identifying one from another.

She ran through all the ceremonials she knew, did the Form of the Fish and the Form of the Hexagon (with points) as she walked, and in one of her more inspired moments invented the unabbreviated Form of the Hexagon (with Fishes as points).

There was hope, at times a castle in the distance. And there were always the recursive shadows, drawn to the bulb-shaped scent that clung to her.

But most of all, and for the longest time, there was being alone.

***

The visitor left a trail of cut blossoms and bloodstains and not one of her Swords could stop them.

Bas had not named a new Blade after sending Fel Valens to the mirror world. It hadn't felt right. And Bas had lasted. Weeks, almost a month even. But it was late into spring, and seeing the warrior cut through her defenses like they were low clouds, Bas almost wished she had.

But, even if it had come to this, Bas would not have unnecessary bloodshed.

She told her enchanters and acolytes to hide, told the Swords and Daggers to guard them and not to worry, and walked down to greet the newcomer unprotected.

"It's you." Bas stopped stock-still in the middle of the High Enchanter's hall, hand over her throat, covering her soul. "Val."

The shape bowed. Its clothes were clotted with dried blood, mirror denizen and human. There was so much of it that Bas had only known it was Fel because of the crown of lantern flowers. Fel's sword arm was encrusted with diamonds and quartz clusters binding her armor and blade to her body, and she held something else in her other hand, but Bas couldn't tell what.

Above them, wreaths of peonies hung their heavy heads.

"I should have listened to you." Bas exhaled, and then laughed. "All my advisors are dead. Monsters got them."

The day before yesterday, the mirror creatures had stopped entirely. No surface lured them out, and her adepts whispered that it must have been the Queen, the unquestioned authority of the mirror world, who called off the assault. Maybe Fel Valens had negotiated a truce. Maybe they were free.

No reply, no movement from Fel. Bas swallowed. "Tell me what happened."

The other girl raised the object that she had in her not-sword hand and tossed it toward Bas. It rolled unevenly, like it had been carved by an unskilled artisan, and gave off discordant chimes in its wake, gleaming when light hit its planes.

When it stopped by Bas' feet and silence fell again, she recognized it. Severed glass, translucent hair, and lifeless diamond eyes frozen in an attitude of horror. "The Queen of All Mirrors."

"The Mirror Queen." Fel inclined her head. On her brow, somehow nestled between her hair and the lantern flowers, jutted a crown of diamonds and jagged beads of glass.

Bas knew each of the seven spells for shattering by heart, had them etched into her memory by the scriptorium's instructors from age ten on just in case she should find herself in exactly this position, but in that moment she couldn't cast any of them.

And maybe Fel was remembering the same things Bas was, the sticky summer days, dew-bright roofs at dawn, the vows binding them as Blade and High Enchanter, because she didn't raise her sword against Bas. Instead, she mechanically cut the opening letters of a portal into the dais floor, her writing coming out in clumsy, untutored slashes. It did not matter. She was the Mirror Queen, and the magic answered.

"Why did you even come back?" Bas yelled. She snatched a vase of flowers from the sideboard and threw it to the ground. "Just to show me this?"

Fel looked at the snapped stems and then at Bas like she really ought to know the answer, shrugged, and scythed the circle to completeness.

"Val, wait." Bas dashed forward, calling on every bit of magic she could. "Don't—"

Fel held the sword up as the portal yawned open in the same spot as it had weeks before and then halted. The floor beneath her had turned to mirrors, and around her wrist a ragged carnelian ribbon fluttered. "Do not."

Peonies split into broken globes of pink and oxblood, flowers peeled themselves open in Bas' veins, and a single coda of a horoscope slashed itself into a leaf.

"I just, I wanted—" The portal rippled, a tear slid down her cheek, and at last, Bas let go. "I'm sorry."

Bas could have sworn that Fel's eyes wavered. But no, that was impossible, for they too were made of glass. "I," Fel said, before she vanished back into the mirror world she held dominion over, leaving Bas only with dead marks hewn into an empty hall, a thousand ruined flowers, and a gleaming head, "am not."

SCRAP METAL

Tara Calaby

Tara Calaby is a a British-Australian writer, currently living in Melbourne, Australia. She holds a Master of Arts in ancient history and is studying towards a Master of Letters in creative writing. Her work has appeared in Daily Science Fiction, Aurealis and Suddenly Lost in Words. When not writing or studying, she can be found researching her family tree or attempting to learn Welsh.

Mae woke to a white light and the sound of her mother's sobbing. The blankets were heavy on her chest and there was a faint scent of something acrid in the air. Her head hurt and her body felt bloated and unsure. It was daytime. The windowpane was speckled with fingerprints but, beyond the glass, there were leaves and branches and a white winter sky.

The room was new to her, but her mind was too fogged for Mae to question it. The fluorescent light stung her eyes. "Mum?" Mae's voice was dry, but the word filled the room.

The sobbing stopped. There was a scrape of chair legs on linoleum and then warm hands pressed against Mae's cheeks and a sequence of kisses marked her forehead. "My baby," her mother said, her mascara smudged prettily in the corners of her eyes. "My poor, poor baby."

Mae tried to move, but her arms and legs felt heavy. Blinking to focus, she looked down at the hands that lay crossed on her chest, like a corpse laid out in a coffin. A thick bandage was wrapped around one elbow. Below it, the skin was silvery and free of markings. A prosthetic, she realised, the thought coming to her as though from a distance. Legs too, most likely. And, through the mist, came a vague echo of screaming brakes.

She was too tired to panic. She slept.

***

When Mae woke again, the room was quiet and she was alone. A grey blind had been lowered over the window and the room was lit only by the cold light that seeped through the open doorway to the corridor. The faint murmur of a distant television was the only sound that penetrated the silence.

There were footsteps in the corridor, and the room darkened as a sturdy body paused at Mae's door. "You're awake."

The overhead light flicked on and Mae closed her eyes against the sudden glare. When she dared open them, she recognised a nurse's uniform.

"You're a lucky girl," the nurse said. "You've been fitted with the very best cybernetic prosthetics available. Dr. Olssen is a leader in the field."

"But—" Mae paused for a moment, trying to clear the fog in her mind. "There's a waiting list. It's always in the news."

"You have excellent connections."

Mae understood. "My mother."

"A good friend of Dr. Olssen," the nurse said, her smile tight. "Now, can you lift that cup beside your bed?"

To Mae's surprise, she was able to do so effortlessly, the prosthetic hand acting just as her biological hand would have done. If anything, it was easier; there was a mechanical strength in the new hand that made the glass seem almost weightless.

"As I said, you're very lucky. A bit of rehab and you'll be back to normal in no time."

Normal, Mae thought. Nothing will be normal again.

***

When Mae's mother returned, she was not alone. Mae ordered the photographers out of her room in a voice so loud that a nurse came to investigate the noise.

"Really, Mother?" she said once they had gone.

Loretta smoothed the perfect lines of her suit. "I didn't think you'd mind, dear. Dr. Olssen has been good to you. I thought you'd be pleased to give him some publicity."

"Give you some publicity, you mean." Mae shook her head. "I won't play crippled daughter to give you a boost in the polls."

"Such a cynic." Loretta checked her reflection in the window. "You get that from your father. The public loves stories about cybernetic enhancement; it's only fair to satisfy that need."

"I'm hardly enhanced," Mae said. "I walk like a robot and my hand keeps twitching."

"You can't expect to adapt instantly. Why must you always be so negative?"

Mae took a breath before replying. "I'm a triple amputee. I think some negativity is justified."

"You were a triple amputee," Loretta corrected her. "I wasn't about to let you languish in the public system for years."

"Yes, about that." Mae held her mother's gaze. "I've seen the news reports. The waiting list for these things is ridiculous. And yet…here I am."

Loretta smiled. "Never underestimate the power of wealth, dear."

"But money can only go so far," Mae persisted. "They can't make enough prostheses to satisfy demand. Everyone knows that. Your own government set up the training grants."

Loretta dismissed her with a wave. "They always hold back a few for VIPs. It's how the world works. How many times have we eaten at fully-booked restaurants because of who I am?"

"Food's different to these hunks of metal." Mae raised her right arm. The sun's light was entering the room at just the right angle to emphasise the silvery sheen of its skin. As Mae rotated her hand, the metal joints moved in a way that was almost human and she resisted a shudder of disgust.

**

Rehabilitation wasn't as difficult as Mae had imagined. Once the worst of the pain from the implantations had faded, she was met in her room every morning by a physiotherapist. For the hand, he taught Mae repetitive exercises that strengthened the synthetic links between the prosthesis and her brain. She spent hours writing and rewriting the letters of the alphabet, the letters slowly becoming more legible with time. Keyboards were easier, as they didn't require the same fine motor skill, although Mae's left and right hands didn't coordinate as well as before and the letters occasionally jumbled on the screen.

While the therapist also showed Mae leg exercises aimed at improving her balance, he emphasised that walking was the key to adaptation. To that end, Mae was instructed to spend as much of her day as possible roaming around the public areas of the hospital.

Three Pine House, Mae learned, had originally been a private home, and much of the hospital was still housed within the old mansion. Bold signs directed those seeking cosmetic surgery up the front staircase to the first floor, and most of the patients' rooms were located in the mansion's heavily renovated left and right wings. Beyond the original part of the building, there was a sizeable extension, all glass and white paint and stainless steel. It was here that Mae did much of her walking. The floor-to-ceiling windows gave a near-interrupted view out to the garden, and the corridors were wide and sympathetic to Mae's awkward gait.

There was a sterility in the new part of the building that went beyond the usual hospital smell of disinfectant and welding propane. The white-clad nurses blended into the white walls and the white sunlight reflected off the silver-white steel. When Mae walked down the halls, the nurses nodded to her but did not speak, almost as though they too were part of the backdrop.

The old part of the hospital was different. The corridors were narrow and the floorboards—although stained and polished—creaked under the increased weight of Mae's legs. The walls were still white, but the windows were smaller and fewer, and the light never carried to the corners of the high ceilings. There, the nurses were often hidden away, in patients' rooms or offices, and the smell was one of age: of crumbling and concealment.

And so she preferred to leave the left wing for the glass and metal of the extension, and her regular walks always took the same path. On the fourth afternoon, however, Mae closed the door to her room behind her, and her legs carried her in the opposite direction.

Mae had grown used to strange twitches from the new limbs, which the nurses reassured her were a normal part of the brain's adjustment, but occasionally things happened that made her wonder whether she had any control over the prostheses at all.

That sensation was only heightened, Mae discovered, when your legs seemed to have a mind of their own. Her attempts to turn just caused her to wobble feebly, her torso too weak to redirect the greater weight and power of the metal-filled legs. She grabbed at a nearby doorway with her left hand, but it only stilled her for a moment before the grip was broken. She thought about calling for a nurse, but the absurdity of the situation kept her silent.

By then, Mae had reached the end of the corridor and had passed beyond the grand front staircase and into the murkier administration area behind it. There, the hall was narrower and lit only by yellow fluorescent lights. The offices were cramped and uninviting; Mae caught glimpses of desks as she passed. At the end of the hall was a door with a sign on it that read Strictly Staff Only Beyond This Point. Mae's legs paused and she had a brief moment to feel relieved before her right hand reached out to turn the knob.

"Can't you read?"

Mae turned—and now my body decides to obey me, she thought—and recognised the matron by her grey uniform and grey-streaked hair. "I'm sorry, matron," she said, aware of how crazy she must sound, "but I'm having trouble controlling my prostheses."

The matron regarded her through narrowed eyes, as though trying to assess whether Mae was being wilfully ridiculous or merely lying. "That would be highly unusual," she said briskly, "but I suppose I can ask Dr. Olssen to look in on you when he next has a free moment."

Mae's cheeks were hot. "Thank you," she said. "That would be good."

The matron watched as she walked away. Mae's legs did as she wished and, when she reached her bedroom, she buried her face in her pillow and cried.

***

Dr. Olssen was not the tall, fair young man that Mae had imagined. Instead, he was middle aged, with greying black hair and a weak jaw. His clothes were noticeably expensive, but he didn't carry himself like Mae's mother or her friends. He didn't look Mae in the eye when he spoke, instead staring at her breasts or focussing on a point above her head.

"Matron tells me you have a complaint about your prostheses," he said by way of greeting, taking the folder from the shelf beside Mae's bed and flicking through it too quickly to read more than the occasional word.

"I wouldn't call it a complaint."

He didn't look up. "No?"

"I've just been finding that I have no control over them at times."

"Some weakness at first is only to be expected."

Mae frowned. "Weakness isn't the issue. They're strong. Very strong. I've no way of stopping them when they decide to do what they want."

Olssen looked up briefly, huffing with disdain. "They don't want anything, Miss Robson. They're inanimate objects, given movement through your brain's commands."

"If that's right, then something is going wrong with the connection to my brain."

Olssen replaced the folder, taking Mae's right arm instead. With the bandage removed, the join between her body and the prosthesis was a red, shiny band of skin dotted with dark stitches. The healing wound looked untidy against the contrast of the silvery hand.

"Everything looks good to me," Olssen said, rotating the wrist. "The synthetic skin is particularly nice on this model, and the joints are all working smoothly. Occasionally, we see problems with the metal structure—we're dealing with such minute details, you see—but in this case we were able to integrate the new and old skeletal systems with no difficulty. It's always easier with young, fit patients such as yourself."

"Then why do my legs and my hand do what they want?" Mae persisted.

"It's very normal to experience the occasional twitch at first. Just as the join sites need to heal, so do the new connections we've made to the brain."

Mae laughed. "Twitches? Are you trying to say that my legs twitched me halfway around the building?"

Olssen met Mae's eyes for the first time since entering her room. "No," he said. "Miss Robson, I am telling you that it just isn't possible for prostheses to do that. The technology is amazing, yes, but it's only a tool: a tool that you command."

"I know what I experienced."

"You've had a hard time of it." Olssen patted her on the shoulder, his hand lingering longer than necessary. "It must be difficult, adjusting to your new body. But you've been given a great opportunity."

Olssen's round, smug face was really beginning to annoy Mae. "So I should shut up and be grateful that my mother is powerful enough to push me to the head of the queue?"

Olssen smiled. His teeth were perfect and unnaturally white. "Cybernetic limbs are incapable of movement without a command from a human brain. You are either lying or mistaken. If you like, I can arrange for the hospital psychologist to pop in to discuss your feelings of loss relating to your injury—and your feelings of guilt about qualifying for private care."

Mae closed her eyes for a moment and took a breath before replying, a technique learned and perfected in twenty-seven years of knowing her mother. "No, thank you. I'm not lying, and I'm not crazy. I know my body and I know when something is wrong with it."

"The offer will be there if you change your mind." Olssen obviously didn't believe a word she was saying. "And, in the meantime, please stay in the public areas of the hospital. The private areas are not as well maintained, and may be unsafe."

"I'll do my best," Mae said, her upper lip twitching slightly as the doctor left the room.

***

The next time it happened, it was late at night and the corridors were quiet and abandoned. Mae was woken by her legs sliding out from under the bedclothes and her right hand raising her torso from the mattress. The room was lit only by the faint line of moonlight seeping under the base of the Holland blind. Mae's mind was dull and clumsy with sleep, but she was aware enough to feel frightened, and to clutch at the sheets with her left hand as her body rose.

Mae's efforts were unsuccessful, the sheet tugging free of the mattress and trailing uselessly on the floor behind her as her legs carried her over to the door and out into the hall. Feeling even more conspicuous with the sheet hanging like a security blanket from her hand, she let it drop. She turned her head once before her legs took her around the corner, and the discarded fabric looked like a corpse in the shadowy hall.

Her legs took Mae straight to the older part of the hospital. Here, the lights were even weaker, away from the patients and the nurses' offices. The grand staircase looked like a felled tree in the silent foyer, and the solid wood doors to the grounds were closed and presumably locked. For the first time, Mae realised that she was kept at Three Pine House by more than her rehabilitation. Her stomach twisted.

Abandoned by its staff, the administration corridor was dark and cool. The only light was provided by the green glow of the exit sign above the doorway to the foyer. In the darkness, the hall felt even narrower, the walls grey and close at Mae's sides. Worried that she might trip, Mae groped along the walls for a light switch but, if one existed, it was out of her reach. Her lack of vision didn't seem to impede her movement, however. Her legs carried her to the far end of the corridor without incident, and her right hand hung, motionless, at her side.

It was only when she reached the door marked Staff Only that the hand twitched and rose, its movement jerky as it reached out and turned the handle. The door was not locked, and it opened smoothly and silently to reveal another green-tinged darkness beyond. Here, there was a switch right beside the door, and fluorescent light burned Mae's eyes as the shadows of the hall flickered out of view.

Dark, peeling wallpaper covered the walls and the carpet underfoot was worn completely bare in places. Original features, a real estate agent would call it but, to Mae, it looked like the putrefaction of many years. There were spider-webs on the cornices and a smell of mildew in the air. Mae shivered, and not just from the cold.

She was moving slowly now, as though the wing was unsettling her prostheses too. On the right, she passed an open door that led to a room with a crumbling chaise lounge and wooden floors. Heavy curtains pooled at the base of windows that were covered in mouldering planks of wood. Mae was glad when her legs passed the room without pausing.

At the end of the hall, there was a heavy wood door, with a faded KEEP OUT sign nailed slightly off-centre. Mae felt her throat tighten as her right hand attempted to turn the handle, but the door remained closed. Locked, she thought, relieved, but her hand rattled the knob for some time before stilling.

There was the sickly smell of decay in the air. Mae's legs gave way, and she crumpled to the floor.

***

"You've always had a big imagination." Mae's mother stood near to the door, the perfect picture of I can't stay long. "You used to scare your sister half to death talking about monsters."

"That was a long time ago. This is real." Mae didn't like crying in front of her mother, but today the tears refused to stop. "I'm scared."

"Don't be silly." Loretta retrieved a packet of tissues from her handbag and passed them to her daughter. "You're in a hospital: the safest place in the world! And, if there are any problems, you're surrounded by people who can help."

As if he had heard her, Dr. Olssen walked into the room, a suit jacket folded over one arm and his hair slicked back. He deposited the jacket on Mae's bed as he was motioned into Loretta's wide-spread arms. "The nurses told me you were in today," he said into her shoulder, his body pressed close against her breasts. "Always a pleasure, Lottie. Always a pleasure."

As Mae wrinkled her nose in response to the display, her right hand reached into the pocket of Olssen's jacket, slipping back under the bedclothes with a silvery tangle of keys clutched within its fist.

Mae opened her mouth, but remained silent.

* * *

Mae was not surprised when her legs woke her again that night. Her hand found the keys where it had hidden them— a half-eaten packet of biscuits beside Mae's bed—and folded its fingers tightly around them, so that there was no chance of Mae prising them from its grasp. She was not sure she wanted to. As fearful as she was, she felt like she had embarked upon a journey, and a part of her wanted to know where she'd end up.

Her legs took the same route as the previous night. Again, Mae found herself in the formal foyer, and again she passed along the office-lined corridor and through to the dilapidated area beyond the forbidding door. There, however, she stopped, as though her limbs were sharing her apprehension.

The nights were getting colder, and Mae was dressed only in her pyjamas. There was a chill in the musty air that raised her skin into goosebumps and caused her to shiver. The silence in the mouldering wing was unbroken and oppressive. Mae's legs began to walk.

As she approached the door, her right hand rose, fumbling with the keys. Mae could see that there were not many on the ring. One was easily identifiable as a car key, and several looked decades too modern to fit the rusting lock. Only two were the right shape and age, and Mae's hand fit the first into the keyhole without difficulty. She found herself hoping that the key wouldn't turn, but it was the right key and the bolt slid back quietly. Mae closed her eyes as her right hand opened the door.

Her curiosity was greater than her fear. Even once she opened her eyes, the room remained dark, but there was a light switch beside the door. Once illuminated, the room quickly revealed the reason for its blackness: it was large and window-less, the only other break in the wallpaper being a door on the far wall. The condition of the wallpaper was better than in the hall, and Mae could see that the room had once been beautiful. There was a long table in front of her, its surface covered in dust, and chairs that bled their stuffing onto the floor. There were worn rugs and bookcases and darkened paintings on the walls, but most of all there was the smell. It was sweet and it was sickening and Mae retched as the foul air filled her lungs.

"So that's where my keys went." Dr. Olssen was beside her before she'd registered the sound of his footsteps. "Trespassers are not tolerated in this hospital, no matter who their mothers may be."

"I'm sorry," Mae said, a twisting heaviness filling her chest. "My hand—"

"Oh please. Spare me the fairy tales." Olssen tried to take the keys from Mae's hand, but the metal of her fingers was immovable. "You damn cyborgs are more trouble than you're worth. How much do you know?"

"I don't understand."

"What have you seen?"

Mae followed Olssen's gaze to the closed door. "Only this room." Her right hand shook the keys, causing them to jangle.

"You're lying." Olssen's face was tight with anger and something that looked like fear. "You society types are so quick to expect special treatment, but you never think about what has to happen for you to get it. And then you find out the truth and blame the very people who got you what you wanted. Do you think it's easy for me? I got into this business to heal people, but there's no money in waiting lists and wheelchairs."

Mae tried to back away, but her legs remained stationary. "If you need money, my mother—"

"Tempting, but no. You'd talk." Snatching a thick book from the bookcase beside him, he swung it at Mae. It connected at the temple, dazing her, but her stance remained firm and motionless, and her right hand did not flinch. Olssen raised the book again. "At least you'll be good for spare parts."

"Stop! I don't know what you're talking about," Mae pleaded, her head already beginning to pound. "I won't talk. I won't tell anyone you hit me. I don't want to be here at all. If you help me, I'll go. I didn't mean to trespass."

Olssen ignored her. As he attacked again, Mae's right foot knocked his legs from beneath him. His knees made a dull sound as they met the tapestry rug and his eyes grew wide as Mae's right hand stretched forward and thrust the car key into the side of his neck.

The doctor's blood was dark and quick-flowing. He clutched at his neck, trying to close the wound, but the key had torn a jagged hole in his flesh and his fingers were soon coated as the blood continued to pool on the floor.

"What can I do?" Mae asked, her throat tight and sore. She tried to go for help, but her legs would not comply.

Olssen did not reply, focussed only on the lake of red in which he was kneeling. When he crumpled sideways, his eyes closing, Mae felt the cold of the room inside her veins.

"You've killed him!" she shouted, hitting her right hand with the left, ignoring the pain of the metal beneath her fingers. "You've killed him and I'll go to jail!"

Mae's tears came in a wave, the situation crashing over her as she struggled to draw breath.

***

It was a long while before Mae's legs moved again. Her tears had all but subsided and she had fallen into a dazed state, barely registering as she approached the door on the far wall. The car key was covered in Olssen's blood, but it was the second of the old keys that her right hand slid into the keyhole, and it opened the lock freely, as though it was frequently used.

As the door opened, the smell became almost unbearable. The inner room was dark, and this time it was her right hand that felt for the switch. The light was dim, but it was enough to turn the shadows into a gallery of corpses. The bodies were lying discarded on the floor, their missing limbs reminiscent of ancient statues. It was colder in the room—very cold—but not cold enough. The smell was a living thing. Mae retched, and then vomited onto the floor beside what once had been a head.

Mae's legs carried her to the far corner of the room. She stared with dull eyes at the mottled female body that lay before her. Like most of the corpses, it was beginning to decompose. It was missing its legs and the lower part of its right arm. Above each wound was the familiar pink scar of the prosthetic surgery that had taken place. Mae's legs knelt beside the body, and her right hand stroked red hair back from the remains of the woman's face. She looked down at her arm and at the silvery lines of her legs. They must have been a perfect fit.

MAN-FRUIT

Clara Kiat

Clara Kiat grew up in the
Philippines and lives in Manila.
This is her first publication.

Sisinia is six moons away from giving birth. She is barely showing but a practiced eye like Puring's could tell that the child held fast to its mother's innards. A clingy, stubborn child. She kneads Sisinia's lower abdomen until the child takes shape just beneath the skin of the womb. It is as big as her fist. Puring cups it between her palms with the same affection a potter has for a lump of clay. At Sisinia's signal she squeezes and pinches. Her hands are gnarled but her grip is fearsome. This is the ideal time, Puring thinks, when the bones have not yet fully formed.

When Puring is finished she wipes the damp hair from Sisinia's forehead. "You will start to bleed tonight and it shall be gone by morning." She shuffles to the kitchen to brew ginger tea while her patient lies still on the mat. Sisinia waits for the daggers in her vitals to relent and the torment subsides to a dull, tolerable ache.

When it is time to leave Sisinia offers Puring a few pesetas and a burlap sack from which a plump hen emerges in a flurry of feathers. It squawks in protest, its vermilion eyes radiating hate. "Supper," Puring says with a wan smile as she stuffs the bird back into the sack.

In the evening Puring makes her way to Sisinia's hut. She skirts the main road to town and wends her way through the thick woods. She can sense the dying breath of the dry season in the humid night air, and in a matter of weeks it will give way to the damp exhalations of the monsoon. The treetops are awash in pallid moon glow but underneath the dense forest canopy a black void simmers beyond the reach of light. Puring's eyes are accustomed to the dark and she moves along steadily, cautiously. What explanation could she – an old woman wandering about in the deep of night – offer to the guardia, for whom no Indio was above suspicion? Violation of the curfew would mean spending a most unpleasant night in the town jail.

A decrepit plaza sits at the heart of the pueblo. At the turn of the seventeenth century the first Castilians hacked their way through the jungle, rounded up a settlement of Indios, and established the parish. From there the pueblo was born. Two and a half centuries later, the plaza had abandoned its pretensions to stately magnificence, surrendering to neglect and to the punishment of the tropics. Every structure is scarred with mementos from earthquakes and cyclones. The plaza's missing cobblestones remind one of a child's grin. A stone obelisk at the center of the plaza commemorates the valiant deeds of some Castilian monarch but the engraving has long since faded or was defaced by a disgruntled subject. The governor's mansion calls to mind an orgulous, ailing dame held back from collapse by the flimsiest skeins of pride. Behind the old church – built out of the volcanic vomit that abounds in these parts – lies a sprinkling of thatched huts.

Sisinia's hut is propped a few feet above the ground on bamboo poles as large as a man's thigh. Placing both palms and the sole of her right foot flat against the thatch, Puring scales the wall. She is approaching the rooftop when a foot misses its mark, and for a moment she hangs on to the thatch, her legs suspended in the air. From within the hut someone lets out a low groan. Puring feels the beginnings of an agitated flapping in her insides. She used to be much nimbler and sure-footed. With great effort she heaves herself up and crawls to the rooftop.

Puring glances up at the sky and determines that she has a few more hours until moonset. With her fingernails she pokes a small hole through the roof and lowers her long, thin, hollow tongue through the opening. The sharp point of her tongue pierces the swell of Sisinia's belly. It triggers only the slightest discomfort, like the bite of an ant, and Sisinia hardly stirs. Puring makes quick work of the child within. She had kneaded well. It is like fruit that had been macerating in wine. A small belch escapes from her lips. Like a tick engorged with blood she unlatches herself from the roof and springs down noiselessly to the ground. Humming softly, Puring disappears into the woods.

***

Sisinia had married him out of obligation. To settle an old debt her parents had given her hand to Espiridion. Her parents tilled the fields that belonged to the governor and when he claimed more tribute than what he was owed, her parents maintained a helpless silence. To speak out would be folly and to claim recourse to justice would invite the governor's ire. As it was, Espiridion offered some reprieve. He had inherited a bit of farmland from a distant relative. It was not much but it was considerably more than what Sisinia's family had, which was nothing. Espiridion offered the field for her parents to till. With the land Espiridion also acquired the airs of a señor. He reminded his neighbors to address him as Don Espiridion. He insisted on taking a cup of hot chocolate for breakfast, as the Castilians and the rich mestizos were wont to do, rather than the humble ginger tea that his neighbors subsisted on.

Despite his pretensions Espiridion is coarse of tongue, quick of fist, and has a weakness for palm wine. The thought of bearing his children instills deep fear in Sisinia. She would never live with the shame of propagating Espiridion's line. Puring had been surprised when Sisinia, then a frightened sixteen-year-old, came to see her, for no wife gets rid of her first fruit. Very quickly Puring understood the reasons for Sisinia's distress. She could identify fathers from the scent of the unborn and Sisinia's issue exuded an aroma of tobacco, palm wine and spite. She put an end to all seven of Sisinia's subsequent pregnancies.

No one suspects Puring of being anything other than an old, prudent midwife – and to those whose pregnancies she quietly terminated, she is lauded as a discreet and eminently reliable masseuse. No one knows about her nocturnal visits. They do not know that she can smell man-fruit in their wombs. Her rule is simple: she can only feed on discarded man-fruit. She hides among them in plain sight knowing that they would torch her alive should her secret slip out.

There had been an accident, once, in her early years. Her tongue had punctured deep in the patient's womb and caused her to bleed to death. Puring did not realize it until morning when loud keens erupted from the woman's hut. She joined the anxious throng that gathered around the body, which lay on a mat with its hair streaming out like the tendrils of some dark, malevolent plant. Its right eye was slightly open. No one else saw it, but the eye twitched ever so imperceptibly and turned its gaze on Puring. Overcome with horror and guilt, she ran out of the hut. For a long time she did not venture out to feed.

***

During her mother's final years, Puring kept her alive with bovine fetuses. At night Puring roamed her neighbors' fields in search of pregnant carabao. She left them bereft of off-spring and at daybreak a murder of crows fed upon their slit bellies. She wept for each animal that she slaughtered.

"I have had enough," her mother said one night after Puring hauled in a warm, pulsing sac.

"But you must," insisted Puring.

"You fear what comes after I am gone. There is nothing to be afraid of. You must let me go."

Her mother had lived far too long. Puring knew that the time had come but she did not want her mother's gift. She did not want to feed on man-fruit as her mother did. She wanted to live a life free of terrible secrets, without fear of hurt at the hands of her neighbors. And doing so would mean her mother languishing in a state of uncertainty.

The mother regarded her sobbing daughter with a helpless pity. She, too, had reluctantly gone through the same transformation years ago. She herself had been a midwife and, after receiving the gift from her own mother, she eventually devoted her practice exclusively to women who wished to terminate. She waited until Puring ran out of tears. In the ensuing silence she began heaving and retching. The sounds reminded Puring of a choking cat. Before she could look away, her mother reached into her throat and, to Puring's horror, plucked out a tiny bird the color of charcoal.

"You must swallow it whole."

The bird wriggled in Puring's grasp. Nothing about it seemed unusual except for its eyes that gleamed like obsidian. The eyes had no sclera at all. She thought of her many forebears who had borne this bird within them. Most had been fortunate to avoid scrutiny but a few had been driven out by the Castilian friars, who called on their god while holding back angry villagers armed with machetes. There was a great-grandmother who barely survived a whipping with stingray tails. As far as Puring knew, no one had broken the line.

Her mother stretched out a searching hand and Puring realized that she had gone suddenly, inexplicably blind.

"Please, Puring. You know that I cannot die until it is in you."

The bird made strange ticking noises as it slipped down Puring's throat. It clawed at her with its little talons and the taste of blood flooded her mouth. Strange things were happening to her tongue: it twisted about, rolled unto itself, thrashed like a fish stranded on shore.

Puring held her mother's hand until she was gone. As she bent to kiss her forehead she saw that the entire surface of her mother's eyes had turned a shiny, dark gray. It was as though she was looking into a mirror and she was puzzled to see that her reflection was inverted. She ran her hand over her mother's eyes. With the eyes closed, Puring could only interpret the expression on her mother's face as one of gratitude.

***

Espiridion is infuriated by his wife's miscarriages. Since inheriting the land he had been anxious for progeny, and with a young, lissome wife like Sisinia he expected to father a big brood. After ten barren years he is beginning to worry that he may be cursed. He is irked by his neighbors' subtle mockeries. He is older than Sisinia by more than two decades and any fault would be perceived as his.

"I've been rutting you like a bull and you give me nothing in return," he yells at his wife.

"It is not my fault that you have poor seed," Sisinia shouts back. Nothing can be farther from the truth but she must take care to put the blame on him. Espiridion's seed resisted all manner of intimate infusions and crude pessaries. What misfortune to be married to a fiend, and one with such prolific loins.

"How is it my fault if your womb is full of thorns?"

"Very well, then. I hope it shreds your thing to pieces."

His fist lands on a choice spot. She leans against the wall until the room stops spinning. Her tongue informs her that a tooth has gone loose. She spies the empty water jug resting on one of the kitchen shelves. The smirk on Espiridion's face vanishes as the jug hurtles in his direction. It comes crashing to the floor. Without taking his eyes off Sisinia, he bends down to pick up a shard and flicks it at her.

In the afternoon he returns home early from the fields. He seizes her from behind and pins her to the ground. She paws around wildly for something to hit him with. The ferment on his breath makes her stomach curdle.

"Why can't you love me," he whines. A thick trail of his spit trickles down her nape.

***

When pickings are slim Puring travels to neighboring pueblos, knocking on doors under the pretense of selling herbal remedies. She makes friendly overtures to pregnant women, plants doubts in the minds of the most vulnerable, and drops discreet mention of her skill. She is ashamed of her deceit, but, she concludes, she would rather engage in such manipulation rather than feed on someone's womb without some sort of permission. The Castilians are largely to blame for her troubles. Man-fruit is scarce in pueblos where the men are called away to build churches and bridges for the Castilian lords. Puring finds herself venturing out more often to other pueblos. The travel wears her out. She would have to find a willing heir while she is still capable. The thought fills her with dread.

There are others like her living in various pueblos and she must seek them out before it gets too late. Now, in her old age she regrets not having children, not for the sake of passing on the gift, but for the joy it would have brought her. A daughter would have been a source of comfort, a confidant, a protector. A daughter like Sisinia. She feels an urge to protect her from her brute of a husband. She could, for a moment, lay aside her principles. How hard would it be to waylay the husband in a dark, lonely road and gut him like the animal that he is?

Puring informs her neighbors that she is going away on a long journey to visit kin. She laughs off their concerns and bids them farewell. She entrusts the care of her little hut to Sisinia.

"Please don't be gone too long," Sisinia whispers as she bends to kiss the old woman's hand.

"I will be back before you know it," Puring gently assures her. She tucks a handful of cigars inside her blouse, wraps her sparse hair in a bright red kerchief, and sets off on her way.

***

It is as Sisinia feared. She is with child again. She curses her fecundity, wondering what sort of alchemy exists between her and her husband's vitals. It is almost as if her womb is in rebellion, furious at her for quelling its very purpose, and persisting in creating yet more life. If only it would be easy to pluck out this cursed organ, be rid of it once and for all. The herbs Puring taught her to use have no power over the creature growing within her. She bears no anger towards this child or to the others. Rather, she is seized with an urge to punish her treacherous body. After Espiridion leaves for the fields she leaps out from the steps of her hut, over and over, until her bones begin to feel like gravel. Blood appears in her underclothes but her joy is short-lived. It slows down to a trickle and nothing else comes out of her.

In a moment of despair she grabs the large, wooden pestle for pounding rice. She manages only one blow. The shock of it knocks her out of her senses.

The child stays put.

Puring's hut remains shuttered.

***

Sisinia decides that it is time to see Manong.

Manong makes a living casting misfortune: spurned love, a string of bad luck, incomprehensible maladies. Espiridion had gone to see Manong when a man claiming to be a cousin appeared in the pueblo and demanded his share of the land. The cousin fell ill and eventually left without pursuing his claim.

"Manong is the very devil, indeed," Espiridion said to Sisinia with the glowering smugness of a man who had successfully thwarted a rival. "But you see, even Satanás himself has a price."

Manong lives on the outskirts of the pueblo near a coconut grove that slopes down the foot of a hill. He glares at Sisinia through the window and does not return her greeting. He is of slight build, stooped with age, and seemingly innocuous, if it weren't for his unsettlingly lush, black tresses. Something about them gives him a minatory air. Sisinia is careful not to look him in the eye to hide her apprehension and to indicate respect – it is unwise to meet the gaze of someone much older.

She is not sure how to bring up her predicament. How would this hostile man react to her plight? She could barely discuss her pregnancies with her own husband. She remembers Espiridion stumbling upon her bloodied skirts and recoiling as if he had stepped on a nest of vipers. She detests Espridion's revulsion even as he has no qualms taking pleasure in her body.

Manong's nostrils flare in indignation at Sisinia's request. "Do you take me for a midwife? You find midwives aplenty in this town but there is only one of me. I do not deal with women's things."

Sisinia holds out a pouch of pesetas that she had carefully

pilfered from Espiridion and Manong's face lights up. This time Sisinia meets his gaze with undisguised contempt.

His hut is a small, one-room affair, and surprisingly sparse. From Espiridion's account of his business with Manong, Sisinia expected a certain dark opulence and evidence of gristly victories. She realizes now that Espiridion may have exaggerated Manong's knowledge of the black arts and the sense of danger that comes with consorting with his ilk. Except for several unlit candles snaking around a mat in the center of the hut, nothing seems out of the ordinary. There are no inverted crucifixes hanging on the walls, no jars of mysterious unguents on the shelves. An oily, herbal tang hangs thickly in the room.

"This is it?" he sputters, incredulous, when he is done counting the pesetas.

"I can come back and bring you something. Rice, a hen or two, vegetables from my garden —"

"Don't bother," he barks, stuffing the coins into his pocket. "I'm not an invalid who needs soup. Lie down and shut your eyes."

As she stretches out on the mat he lights the candles around her. Manong hums in a low monotone. She can feel his hands moving over her body, close enough for her to feel the warmth of his palms. Very slowly he places his hands on the gentle rise of her belly and begins chanting in a language Sisinia does not understand. The heat from the candles suffuses the room with a welcome warmth. The scent of burning wick is oddly comforting. It reminds her of prayers at the altar, of the quiet evenings of her distant girlhood, when her family used to gather around a lamp before retiring to their mats. She feels her body go slack.

His hands slide down and linger in a place where they have no right to be. He stops humming. Her muscles tense and her body braces for violence, a response honed from years of fending off Espiridion's assaults. With a quick push she sends Manong stumbling backwards.

"Swine," she shouts, bolting to her feet. "May the earth swallow you whole, you mud-sniffing pig."

Her foot makes a swift arc and sends the candles toppling to the floor. He cries out what she presumes to be curses in an unknown tongue. His throat catches. What had sounded earlier like ominous invocations have now lost their power, and all she hears now is the whining of a crumbling old fool. She oscillates between regret – for acknowledging his supposed sorcery – and triumph, at the ease with which she ripped off the charlatan's mask. She trains a jet of spit at Manong in an asperges of fury and disgust.

* * *

For once, Espiridion addresses Sisinia with courtesy. He refrains from hitting her. Her silence used to enrage him; now, he pats her cheek as one would do to a sulky child. He makes clumsy efforts to feed her with her favorite foods. Lifting her jaw with a finger, he says softly, "I will take care of you, wife." His eyes shine not so much from sentiment but from the palm wine he had been imbibing in increasing amounts as Sisinia swelled with child.

The moment coincides with a rare summer thunderstorm. The fields are shorn from the harvest and bled dry by the unrelenting April sun. The heat burrows its way with the persistence of a parasite into Sisinia's innermost crevices. Even the child within her lies still. She plants herself by the window, desperate for a breeze. The air, ponderous and unmoving, begins to turn, and Sisinia picks up the scent of the earth sweating. A sharp cracking boom bursts forth from the skies and the deluge pours.

Despite the welcome cool Sisinia feels an intermittent flush.

In the next instant water sluices down her thighs, and she is confused, thinking that the rain had gotten in through the window. A lightning-like stab pierces her lower back.

Espiridion declares that it is impossible to seek out a midwife in the storm and Sisinia, seething with loathing, chooses not to remind him of his terror of lightning. She wants nothing more than a measure of mercy from the heavens, for the caitiff to venture out and be struck dead by a thunderbolt. She collapses on the slatted bamboo floor as Espiridion drops to his knees with the trembling awe of a supplicant appeasing a wrathful deity. The sight of his sour, anxious face, his eyes gaping at the thing that is erupting from her, causes Sisinia's blood to boil.

"Get out," she snarls.

"But Sisinia, our child," he begins to protest. Ignoring the clamping around her hips, she lifts herself up and delivers a kick to Espiridion's jaw. His lip, ample to begin with, bloats like a well-fed leech.

Espiridion's eyes narrow into hateful slits. "Puta."

"You come any closer and I will kill your child."

The room fills with the smell of iron. Sisinia grits her teeth, determined to deny Espiridion the satisfaction of hearing her cry. The effort in of itself saps her strength. She had thought of herself as one accustomed to pain but she is taken aback by the sheer violence of birth. The child slides out of her in one wet gush. The lashes are thick like hers. The mouth is wide like its father's. It is perfect in every way except that it came with the cord coiled around its neck like some regal, imperious jewelry. The silence baffles Espiridion. He grabs the infant by the ankles with the bewilderment of a child struggling with a broken toy.

For a moment Sisinia feels something unloosen within her, some nascent pity for Espiridion and a fleeting guilt for birthing a dead child. The feeling swiftly vanishes when she sees the disbelief and fury on Espiridion's face. Her glance falls on the tiny body. The newborn's coat of white wax reminds her of the heavily powdered harlots who hang around the town jail. Laughter begins as a warm, ticklish itch. The giggles come in fits and starts and soon she is overcome with laughter. She does not remember laughing this hard in her entire life, and this bright surge coursing through her body is the closest she thinks she has ever come to happiness. For what happiness existed in a life like hers? Her girlhood abruptly ended, her youth pawned off to service her parents' debt, her body a vessel for Espiridion's lusts and rages. She remembers her mother's advice on the eve of her marriage to Espiridion. Pleasure follows pain, her mother had said, somewhat consolingly. Sisinia never understood what that meant until now. A strange, intoxicating eupho-ria is washing over her as though her body is rewarding her for withstanding the pain of birth. She locks eyes with Espiridion, takes delight at his stupid, toadish face, and she feels mirth bubble anew within her. The only way to relieve that warm, inner itch is to laugh long and good and hard. It is impossible to stop even as Espiridion's hands close around her throat.

**

Puring leans back against the tree and relishes the warmth from the fading afternoon. She has finished all her cigars and now she wishes she had kept one cigarillo for this moment.

Glistening with her juices, the gray bird writhes on her lap.

The last thing she sees before the curtain descends over her eyes is a large piece of driftwood floating along the marshy river that stretched out in front of her. All her other senses are at their sharpest. She feels the dapple of light through the trees, the shift in the air as afternoon bows down to night, the flitting of winged ants. The gentle lapping of water from the river's edge soothes her. She senses some creature lurking nearby, tasting her through the air with its tongue. Darkness falls around her. The water stirs briefly and she pauses, inclining her head in the river's direction; she hears a splash and all is silent. She lies in wait. They will come, she assures herself, and in their stealth she may not even hear them. Without resistance it will happen quickly. She could have saved herself a long journey had she come to that resolution earlier. She could have bid Sisinia a proper farewell. She could have repaid her for entrusting her fecund body to her care by dispatching the husband to his end. A quick puncture to the heart, unnoticed, and the neighbors will simply blame his demise on years of rough living.

There is a quickening in the river. On her lap the gray bird lets out a strange, almost plaintive, ticking noise.

A FEW MINUTES MORE

L.M. Magalas

L.M. Magalas is excited to
have a story published in
Luna Station Quarterly. Her
fiction has also appeared
in "Cha: An Asian Literary
Joirnal", "The First Line",
and "Twisted Fairy Tales
vol.2". She is thankful for
her family, friends, fiancé,
and fictional creations.

It had all been so simple in the end. She had assumed initially that something or someone would have eventually stopped her. The universe would surely have sent her some kind of sign, a warning not to continue. But it didn't. And when that happened, Susanna realized that if the universe didn't care, then neither did she.

She had done her duty of course. She played through the scenarios, tried to find an alternative. She talked to medical professionals and made peace with her family. But nothing had helped. Nothing had stopped that hollowness she felt, the way her words echoed and rattled around inside her meaninglessly. And so, that afternoon, she had made her way to the Monarchy Bridge. She swung one leg, then another, over the railing, still waiting to feel something, anything, some sense of significance.

And then, she had jumped.

Or had she? The bitter taste of the polluted water had vanished, the burning in her lungs gone. Now, she was in a large, white-walled room with a desk and a single occupant. It was this occupant, the only other person in the room, who spoke first.

"Well, come forward please. I don't want to shout." The voice belonged to an older man, and as Susanna approached the desk, she felt that "older" was an understatement. The gentleman appeared to be on the far side of eighty, his beady eyes peering at her through the folds of his face. The only other distinguishing trait to the man was the few slivers of hair combed across his balding head. He didn't smile. Instead, his eyes nearly disappeared as he squinted at her.

"Are you Miss Susanna Parks?"

"Um…Yes," said Susanna. She shook her head and brushed her hair out her face, trying to focus on the man and not on the fact that her hair was somehow dry. "I'm sorry, but where am I?"

The man frowned up at her, practically swimming in a pale blue suit that was at least two sizes too big for him. "Oh dear," he said. "In a bit of denial, are we?" He pulled closer in his chair and consulted the papers on his desk. "Right then, let's get this done: Susanna Parks, you agree that on November 16th of this year, you committed suicide."

The bluntness of his words coupled with his unfeeling tone made Susanna wince. "Yes," she said, "I did."

"And you understand that as a direct result of your actions, in conjunction with paragraph seven, article thirteen of The Treaty of Life, you are now considered dead."

Susanna shrugged. Apparently she had been successful after all. "I guess so, yep."

"Good, that's done then." The man stamped one of the pages and shuffled them on his desk. "Thank you for not crying and making a fuss. People always do at that part. It does wear on my nerves after a while." He stuck three of the pages in a drawer and pulled out another two. "Now then, the next question, of course, is what to do with your extra days."

Susanna frowned. "I'm sorry," she said. "What extra days?"

The man stopped and looked at her. "Why, your unused days, of course. The ones you would have lived had you not… Has no one told you about this?" Susanna shook her head, causing the man to sigh. "In choosing your own death, you waive the right to use any of your remaining days for yourself, but you are allowed to select a recipient. Understood?"

Susanna shook her head.

The man sighed again, and this time, he stood up. "Right then," he said, tugging on his blue jacket. "Come with me."

The man pressed a button on his desk, and a part of the wall opened to reveal a doorway. The two travelled down a long hallway past other doors, each with a different number. Before Susanna could ask about them, they had come to the door at the end of the hall. This was the last door, and it was here that the man stopped.

"Just a few things before we go in," he said, his eyes nearly disappearing under his furrowed brow. "These people are professionals and their work is very important. It requires a lot of precision and concentration. You're welcome to stare and ask me questions, but don't interrupt them."

"Interrupt who?" said Susanna.

"The Assigners," said the man with a small smile. "And I see the questions have started already."

The man opened the door and the two stepped in. A cacophony of sound met Susanna's ears as her eyes surveyed the scene below her.

To call the scene busy was like calling the Titanic's damage a scratch. It reminded Susanna of the trading floor of the New York Stock Exchange. Hanging from the center of the circular room were monitors and flat screen televisions, showing lists of names and news footage from an endless number of channels. A group of men and women stood underneath, all in black suits, all carrying clipboards, and all of them paying considerable attention to the monitors. Every so often one of them would leave, and Susanna's eyes would follow him or her to one of the many cubicles and desks that circled in two rows around the center of the room. Dozens of people filled these workstations, and were shouting to one another. Susanna felt that she and her guide were the only two people in the room not talking. That was until her guide spoke.

"Welcome to the Intervention Room," he said, with a sweep of his hand to the scene below. "We believe in one thing here: never waste a moment. These are the guys and girls who make sure that it happens. We keep close tabs at all times on ongoing events. Then, we analyze the data and come up with multiple lists of people who may need the extra time. And then we give it to them."

Susanna frowned, her green eyes narrowing. "Let me make sure I understand this. You pick and choose people at random, and you extend their lives? That's playing God. You can't do that."

The man looked at her. "How long did you wait?"

"Excuse me?"

"How long did you wait before you jumped?"

Susanna imagined herself back on the bridge as the man continued. "Five seconds? Thirty? A minute? Most people don't know because to them, time doesn't matter. But to us, it does. It's not always about saving someone's life. Sometimes it's about giving a dying father a few moments to say goodbye to his daughter, or to give the doctors one more minute to save a patient. Sometimes it works, sometimes it doesn't. But think of what the world could do if we just gave it more time. If people stopped wasting their time. That's what the donation of your unused days does. Gives us, all of us, more time."

Susanna was about to speak, but a loud beep began to sound behind them. All eyes went up to the monitor, where there was a breaking story about a shooting. One of the men in black suits quickly consulted his chart and shouted to someone in a nearby cubicle.

"Eight-year-old girl is bleeding out from a stray bullet. Sarah Jenkins of Kawassa, Ohio. Get her up there."

Susanna watched everyone begin to quickly move and scatter like ants. Her elderly guide tugged her arm.

"Come on," he said, pulling her towards the stairs. The two stopped on a lower landing, giving them a clear view of a specific cluster of monitors.

Susanna's eyes scanned the monitors as a live video appeared on the center screen. It was a young girl, and she looked as though she was in pain. Beneath her picture was an odd line pattern that Susanna recognized immediately: her heartbeat.

"What's going on?" asked Susanna.

"Someone needs more time," said the guide, squinting at the screen. "Looks like there was a shooting on her street. A stray bullet has hit her. If she doesn't get help soon, she's going to bleed out."

Susanna felt her heart race. "We have to do something. What does she need?"

"She needs a lot of things," said the guide, "but what she needs most is time." He motioned to the screen, where her picture had been pulled to the front. Various numbers were flashing, and the Assigners in front of the screen were studying them carefully. "Those," said the guide, motioning to the numbers, "are the worst and best case scenario times that she needs. The first time tells us that unless we can get her more time, she's going to die in…seven minutes," he said, checking the clock. "And the police will probably find her two minutes later, judging by our estimates."

"So she needs two minutes," said Susanna.

"She needs more than that," said the guide. "She needs at least five for the police to get her to the paramedics in time, and even then we don't know if they can save her. That's the worst-case scenario. But if we can give her ten, twenty, thirty minutes? Her chances of stabilizing and surviving go up. Now, maybe she dies in surgery. Maybe she doesn't. There's no real guarantee. But for now, the only thing standing between her and definite death is us."

"So save her."

The man looked up at Susanna. "Why?"

Susanna blinked. "Because—because she needs help!"

"So do lots of other people."

"But—she's—" Susanna fought for words. For the first time in a long time, the hollowness in her chest had vanished, replaced by the desperate thumping of her heart. "You need to save her. You have to."

The elderly man peered at her through the folds in his face.

"Now who's playing God?" he asked.

Susanna looked at the picture of the little girl, the clock ticking down next to her. Her hair was in pigtails with those beaded elastics that Susanna remembered from her own childhood. Somewhere, that girl needed help. Susanna felt something ignite inside her.

"Give her mine," she said.

The guide turned. "What?"

"My extra days," said Susanna. "Give them to her. All of them."

The guide began to speak, but a shrill bell overpowered him, and a cheer went up throughout the room.

"Sounds like she's covered," he said, smiling. "We've got enough minutes in the system to get her to the paramedics."

Susanna looked at the screen. The girl's picture had disappeared, but on one of the monitors in the center, a reporter was capturing the discovery of the girl live on camera. She was in critical condition, but she was still alive.

"I take it that you're ready to discuss your unused days now."

Susanna turned to the guide. He was watching her with a curious eye. She nodded.

"Tell me what I have to do."

*****

Beneath all of the papers that the man had on his desk was a calculator. He managed to find it after a few moments, and was punching in numbers and cross-referencing them for a long time. Finally, he looked up at Susanna.

"According to our predictions, you have seven thousand, eight hundred and thirty unused days."

Susanna's mouth dropped slightly. "Really? That long?" she frowned, "I mean, I thought that…" she found herself unable to put her thoughts into words. For the first time, she felt that she might have made a terrible mistake . He noticed her reaction and gave her a sympathetic smile in response.

"You're not the first person to come across my desk with that response," he said. "And you're definitely not the worst case I've seen. I can't help but think that we'd all be happier some-times if we quit letting ourselves get in the way." The man turned the sheet around so that Susanna could read it from her seat on the opposite side of the desk. "In any case, that's how many days you have, which works out to two hundred and sixty-one months, or just short of thirteen years. Which," he said, motioning to the page, "in hours and minutes, works out to this."

"Wow," said Susanna. "That's…"

"Surprising?"

"Intimidating," she said. She slid the page back to him.

The man smiled at the thought, but noticed that Susanna

didn't. In fact, her expression looked sad, her gaze still focused on the paper she'd slid away.

"Something wrong?" he asked.

Susanna looked up and did her best to smile, but the pain was evident. The man waited a long moment and, when she failed to speak up, ventured a guess.

"You want your time back," he said, not sounding entirely surprised.

Susanna didn't respond immediately. "No," she finally said. "It's just…" she floundered for a moment. "It was seeing that girl, her house, her neighbourhood…I never had to worry about all that. I've always had a roof over my head, had family and friends…and all it took was one little hitch, one stupid thing for me to give up on all of it. I couldn't cope. But that girl, she's going through agony, and it's going to make her stronger. Seeing her suffer…it just makes me wish that I hadn't given up." Susanne wiped at her eye quickly before letting out an embarrassed laugh. "I don't even know if I'm making any sense."

"Some," said the man, sitting back in his chair. "You know, I've been on this side of the desk for so long that I've forgotten what it's like on the other side."

Susanna blinked. "So you…you did too?"

The man nodded. "Can't remember why I did it, but I did. And I thought it was such a waste, my time. I didn't do much with it. But when I got here and I saw what these people did, well…I thought this was it. This is what I was meant to do." He looked thoughtfully at Susanna. "We all walk around, impacting others every day with what we say and do without ever fully realizing it. You let someone get in line ahead of you. That changes things. Maybe now they leave the parking lot sooner and they get into an accident at the intersection instead of you. Maybe they don't. We can't know things like that, but accidents happen. We're so connected that if one of us falls, we all, in some way, feel the ripples. That's why I'm here—to stop as many of those accidental disconnects as possible. And the only way I—we—can do that is with the help of people like you."

Susanna was quiet for a moment. Finally she lifted her head and smiled at him through puffy eyes, her face moist. "You're a good salesman," she said.

"Well, I have put in the years," said the man with a gentle wink. He waited a moment before continuing. "So, what will it be? Donating it back into the system? Or have you got someone in mind?"

Susanna leaned forward. "Is that little girl okay now?"

"For the moment," said the man. "We can't predict how long someone will need, what with the human element. But just to be on the safe side, I can set aside some time for her. If she doesn't need it, it'll go back into the system when she passes."

Susanna nodded. "That sounds good."

The man consulted his pages. "A few days are okay?"

"Yes, thank you."

The man jotted something down. "That's been noted. Now that only leaves us with…seven thousand, eight hundred and twenty-seven days left." He gave her a look that was mutually amused and exasperated. "This could take a while, breaking it up into individual recipients."

"No," said Susanna. "Put it all back into the system. If people can use it, let them. But," she said, leaning forward, "is there any way to make sure it's used for kids first?"

The man smiled. "I'll see what I can do."

"Oh, and just one more thing," said Susanna. "I was wondering if you could look up someone for me."

The next hour was a blur, with the two poring over files and signing papers. When it was all done, the man stood up from his desk. Susanna followed suit.

"Well, Miss Susanna Parks of Dormant Street, it was a pleasure meeting you. And on behalf of, well, everyone…I want to thank you for your donation."

"I just hope those minutes are put to good use," she said, "and I have a feeling that they will be."

The man nodded and pushed a different button on his desk. Another part of the wall slid open with another doorway. Susanna looked from the man to the door and back.

"So I guess that's my next stop," she said. Despite her best efforts, her voice was shaking. "Where does it go?"

"I don't know," said the man. "Got recruited for this job immediately after arriving. Apparently there's no accounting for taste around here."

Susanna laughed, her eyes wet. "Any chance you need an assistant?" She swiped quickly at her face. "No, never mind," she said. "It's about time I did something brave."

She made her way slowly across the room, finally stopping just shy of the door. Turning back, she gave the man at the desk a nod. "Thank you," she said, "for everything."

"No, Miss Parks," said the man with a slight bow, "thank you."

"You're welcome," said Susanna, and before she had the chance to change her mind, she stepped through the doorway, and the wall closed behind her.

The man sat back down in his chair and began to tidy up the papers on his desk. He gave a small sigh as he looked at them, the signatures, the recipients. He tried so hard not to get attached, but somehow they always got under his skin. He would just have to try harder.

He had no sooner cleared his desk when the familiar sound

of a 'pop' echoed through the room. A file was on his desk, and the man looked up to see a man in his forties standing there. The man at the desk straightened his back, toughened his resolve, and spoke.

"Well, come forward please," he said. "I don't want to shout."

***

It was a miracle in the midst of a tragedy, the six-month-old baby who had managed to survive. It wasn't the fact that she had survived the collapse of a seven-story building. Nor was it the fact that she had managed to stay alive for more than three days. It was the fact that when the firefighters found her, she was completely unharmed, except for some dehydration. It was something you didn't see often.

***

The paramedics really couldn't believe it. The two-year-old had fallen from a second-storey balcony into the pool below, and had been pronounced dead on the scene. Now they heard that he'd been found breathing in the morgue, right on the examiner's table ready for the autopsy. Things like this just didn't happen in small towns, but the paramedics weren't about to complain. Having to give bad news any day was hard. But this boy had been given more time, and that was the best kind of news.

***

Sarah Jenkins woke up before her alarm, like she did every morning, and got dressed for work. Only today, she had to be careful of her shoulder. An altercation with a suspect had left her with a long, jagged cut down her right arm. Soon it would be a scar. Still, it could have been worse. She'd had time to move back before he attacked. If she hadn't, she'd have been sent to the morgue instead of the hospital emergency room.

She started to put on her uniform shirt, but stopped on the last button. Looking in the mirror, she let her fingers find the familiar spot below her collarbone. The scar was still there. Even after all these years, she could still remember that day—being eight years old, lying on the floor of her living room, and hoping that someone would find her. Thankfully, someone did.

With a small smile, she buttoned up her shirt and reached for her badge. Time to start another day.

WEDDING FEAST

Jessica Lévai

Jessica Lévai is a writer and a former professor who has taught courses in mythology, folklore, and the role of women as creators and disseminators of both. She has been a frequent guest contributor at the blog Overthinking It, where you can find her articles about the anti-monarchial message of Disney's Frozen, and the feminine divine in Transformers: The Movie. She loves stories, music, and comic books.

It was one o'clock on a Thursday afternoon when the bride came in for her final fitting. Violet had brought her mother, Opal, her sister, Sydney, and her maid of honor, Mei, and the four of them were now squeezed into a stall at the back of Ivy's Bridals, waiting for the dress to appear, and sipping the champagne provided by the management. Violet began to undress for the fitting.

"You know," said Mei, "You never told us who you got."

"She didn't?" Syd rolled her eyes. "That's all she's been able to talk about."

Violet placed her carefully folded clothes on a chair in the corner. "Henleigh Asherton. Mei, hand me my shoes?"

"Henleigh?!"

"Shoes!"

Mei put down her champagne flute and retrieved the jeweled flats from the box under her arm. Violet slipped her feet into the flats and looked at them in the mirror.

"I'm sorry, but that's amazing! How did you get Henleigh?"

Sydney answered. "You remember Charice, who was at the shower?" Violet was beginning to shiver in the air conditioning. She peeked around the curtain.

"Yeah."

"Her cousin used Henleigh for her wedding."

Violet drew back into the stall. "I heard it was amazing. Okay, here we go, everyone!" The seamstress appeared at the curtain, bearing the gown over one arm. Opal helped her lift the piles of cream silk organza over Violet's head. Once the zipper was drawn, the seamstress began her last-minute pinning while the wedding party stroked the fine cloth and marveled over the gem decoration.

Mei pulled back from the dress and let out a sigh. "And Henleigh did for Rosalind Smythe when she married Ryder Channing in Ibiza. Remember the pictures?"

Syd helped herself to Violet's untouched champagne. "I remember it set back production on that movie. She couldn't walk for a month."

"But Violet, she's a celebrity! She must be costing you an arm and a leg!" At this, every woman in the room froze, for just a moment, before dissolving into giggles. Even Violet laughed until she was poked by a stray pin. At her daughter's yelp, Opal muttered, "She costs less than the dress."

"Mom, don't start!"

"What?" Opal took an innocent sip of her champagne. "That makes her a bargain. And I still like the A-line."

"It's my wedding, Mother. So I get the dress I want."

"All right."

The seamstress took the momentary pause to demonstrate the bustle, leading Mei through the complicated sequence of hooks and eyes twice. Coming to Violet's side, the seamstress looked the dress over one more time. Violet stared into her reflection, her brow furrowed. "I know it looks a little lopsided," the seamstress assured her, "but this will make it so much easier to navigate with your cane. Oh, you must be so excited!"

Violet seemed to wince. "Right," she said, softly.

The seamstress blinked at this muted response to her

cheerleading. She picked up her pincushion and excused herself, instructing everyone to hang the dress in its bag before leaving. Sydney flicked a fingernail against her empty flute and let the sound hang in the air for a second before saying, "Okay, so let's talk about Sam." Violet looked up at the sound of her groom's name, right into Syd's wicked grin. "How big do you think his is going to be?"

"Sydney!" Opal gasped.

"God, shut up!" Violet scowled, willing the tears back into her eyes. "What is wrong with you?"

"Okay, girls, that's enough," said Opal, briskly unzipping the dress. "Syd, why don't you and Mei go pick up my mother at the airport? Mei, you drive. And you, Violet? Let's have a talk." Mei and Syd left the stall, Mei handing Opal the box for the shoes on her way out.

Violet sank gratefully onto the cushion in the corner. Her mother swiftly nicked the box of tissues, standard in every fitting room, and caught the single tear before it had a chance to land on the gown. The bride silently allowed herself to be dabbed.

"Sweetie, the dress is perfect. It's going to be all right."

Violet took a shuddering breath. "What if it's not enough?"

"The dress?"

"Me!" Another tissue. "What if what I'm offering isn't enough?"

Her mother nodded at this question, then turned her attention to her daughter's shoes. Wordlessly she removed them and placed them gently in their box. Cradling Violet's foot, like when she was a girl, Opal asked, "Is it that you want to change your mind? Do it somewhere else?"

"What, and never wear a bathing suit again?" The blow was

unintended, but it landed all the same. Opal took a tissue for herself from the box. "Mom, I'm sorry, I didn't mean..."

"I made certain choices when I married your father. We both made sacrifices, though. That's how marriage works. Each person gives something. Something precious. Something that can't be taken back. And the bond that's made, it's forever.

"Honey, I know you're scared. But just try to remember that you're not the first person to do this and not the last. We all survived, and you will, too. And your father and I, and everyone, we'll always be there to help."

The hug that followed was heartfelt and much-needed. As the bride dried her tears, she said, "We better go home. Maybe I can take a nap before my appointment with Henleigh."

"Of course. Busy day tomorrow."

***

The afternoon of the wedding finally arrived. The old church was done up tastefully with sprays of flowers and soft candle-light. A string quartet in the corner added the right sweep of romance and reverence to the ceremony.

The groom, Sam, stood before the altar. He was handsome, strong, and looked just a little peakèd. His party the night before had done its job, but then, everyone knew Sam's father could always be counted on for that sort of thing. Despite the ordeal, the groom still radiated excitement for his bride, and all present smiled at the thought of all he would give her.

The quartet struck up a march and the congregation got to its feet with a gentle whoosh, which melted into "aww" as the flower girls, nieces of the groom, dropped clumps of rose petals on the path. Cameras clicked. Mei was next, greeted by the best man at the altar and escorted to her place. As any crowd at a wedding knows to do, all heads turned to see Violet. The bride processed slowly down the aisle, smothered in her cream gown and a delicious vanilla perfume. The cane that supported her had been decorated in another gathering the night before by the flower girls, and shed sugary glitter on the rug with every step. She carried it proudly, a badge of courage, and many of the married women, upon seeing it, thought of their own scars and smiled.

But there's one at every wedding, isn't there?

"I hear it was just a toe."

"Shush, Gramma."

"A toe!" The old woman glanced around for co-conspirators, shrugged at finding none. "A toe. Can you believe it? What is that even supposed to mean?"

"Gramma, enough!"

"It's like she doesn't even want to get married."

The quartet's music faded as the wedding service began, its benign drone more than enough to disguise Gramma's complaint. None other arose. Any objection to the union would have been voiced before. There was already a sort of permanence at work here. The church and the vows were just gravy.

The homily was mercifully short and contained nothing but fine sentiments for the couple, directly from God. The vows the couple recited were simple, beautiful, and to the point. They spoke of fidelity, devotion, and sacrifice. By the time the rings were produced, a scent had begun to waft from the kitchen into the chapel, making mouths water and feet shuffle with impatience. Married couples clasped hands a little tighter in anticipation.

It was time. Murmurs rose from the witnesses as the bride and groom were seated and two carts were rolled into position before them. Susurrations of speculation. The smell was wonderful and boded well. At a signal from the presider, the chapel went silent.

Violet swallowed nervously as she removed the cover and presented the tiny porcelain plate to Sam. Later he would swear to her that he noticed it matched her dress, but right now, all he could see was the morsel before him, the offering of his bride, prepared by none other than Dr. Henleigh Asherton.

Gramma was right; it was a toe. Specifically, it was the left pinky, lovingly braised and spiced, served on a toast square, with a little cream sauce for flavor and effect. Happy tears in his eyes, Sam stood—with some difficulty—and tipped the plate so all could see. Soft, approving noises spread through the crowd, to Violet's visible relief. Sam ate the proffered food in a single bite. It had been small but was perfectly presented and wondrously good, just like he knew it would be. He took her hand and kissed her quickly on the cheek.

The smell from the other cart enticed. The congregation, on the edge of their seats, gasped as the best man handed Sam a knife and fork, which he, in turn, passed to Violet. The cover from the plate before him was removed, and the onlookers burst into applause at its contents.

An ounce! A full ounce, practically a slab, of seared meat! Violet's eyes widened. Hands clapped the shoulders of Sam's father in congratulations. Celebrity doctors were well and good, but everyone knew the old surgeon had the best hands in town. It was a testament to his skill that the boy could even stand!

Violet picked up the utensils and neatly divided the meat in two. One bite, then another, and it was gone. Thunderous applause, again, as the couple embraced. A perfect wedding, with beautiful offerings. There would be happiness, and love, and children.

"I now pronounce you husband and wife," the presider said, unnecessarily. "You are one flesh."

The quartet stuck up again as the families came forward

to escort the new couple to their reception. They were supported, carried, for was that not what the community was for?

The reception followed immediately after the ceremony, as custom dictated. It was a wise tradition. Everyone was so hungry.

ALL THE SOULS LIKE CANDLE FLAMES

Vanessa Fogg

Vanessa Fogg dreams of selkies, dragons, and gritty cyberpunk futures from her home in western Michigan. She spent years as a research scientist in molecular cell biology and now works as a freelance medical writer. She is fueled by green tea. For a complete bibliography and more, visit her website at www.vanessafogg.com. She is erratically active on Twitter at @FoggWriter.

You know of the Sea Witch, of course. Even in your inland towns you've heard her name; you know that she collects drowned souls and keeps them in her cold halls under the sea. All whose bones lie under salt-waves belong to her—merchants and kings, queens and servants, pirates and raiders and innocent babes. Ordinary sailors and fishermen too, of course. Far too many of those from our shores.

You've seen the charms we weave to keep the storms at bay. You've heard the prayers for fair winds and a safe journey home. But what if you're already dead, fishes nibbling through your hair and seaweed twisted 'round your limbs, your flesh dissolving in the cold ocean tides? Who is there then to save your soul from the Witch's black halls?

That's what these charms are for, you see. Go ahead and hold one. Feel how smooth it lies in your hand. It's strong wood, from deeply rooted trees. See how fine the paint job, the black eyes and stripes along the side. No, don't speak to me of those gaudy charms for sale up the street. Mine are truly crafted. See the fine details, the care with which the feathers were made.

Why does a fish have feathers? You really don't know the story of Mikki, do you? I can tell you haven't been here long. No, you can keep ahold of that one. Hold it while I tell you the tale.

***

Years ago this town was scarcely more than a village. Few merchant ships docked at these shores, and fine visitors such as yourselves were a rare sight indeed. But the greatfish still ran in shoals along the coast each spring, and the glittering silveroils ran to the south in the fall. The fishing fleet still set sail each fair day of the season, just as it does today.

There was a family in the village. A little girl who lived with her mother and father and older brother. The mother's true name is now lost, but all in the village called her "Gull". Her clear skin was the white of a gull's breast, and she gathered gull feathers shed on the shore. She washed them in fresh water and wove them into charms for her husband to wear. The gull soars over salt-water but returns to land to nest; so we say that a gull's feathers will guide a seaman home.

It was the first bad luck for the family, when Gull took ill. Until then, it had been a blessed life: the seas fair and the fisherman's nets and lines filled with fish. His wife singing as she fed and clothed and cared for the family. The children growing up, healthy and strong.

Who can say what plague struck the village that year? So many illnesses in this world, fevers and chills of all kinds on this coast. The whole family took ill, coughing and pale, burning and shivering. In this story, the father and children recovered. The mother did not.

They buried her in the grassy field above the village, close to the sun and sky. High and safe from creeping fingers of salt-water, but within sight and smell of the sea. White gulls wheeled and cried above the grave.

So the children were motherless, the daughter still such a tiny thing, barely able to lift the iron kettle above the fire. The boy just a few years older, running wild through the tall dune-grass. Neighbors and relatives tried to help. There was an aunt, the widower's sister. She did her best, but she was busy with her own young children.

The orphaned girl didn't know how to make her mother's feather-charms. She had watched, and her small hands were clever, but there was a knot she couldn't manage, a knack she didn't have. No one else in the village knew how to make them. The girl, who was named Mikki, sat outside her house trying again and again to tie the feathers just so. She cried in frustration, but no one noticed; no one helped.

There was much overlooked the year that Gull died, much that was forgotten.

It wasn't just the charms, or the fish dumplings and soup she had once made. Soon Mikki forgot her mother's face. She could remember other things—a snatch of song, the touch of her mother's hand against her cheek. A fall of dark, silken hair. She remembered sunlight flashing and the sharpness of a rock hurting her foot on the beach, and then crying out to her mother for help. But her mother's face, the shape of her eyes, a distinct image of her—all these were gone.

***

The girl and her brother grew. They learned to take care of themselves. The relatives and neighbors helped out less and less. Mikki and her brother scrambled together over the rocky shore, collecting mussels and seaweed for supper and prying limpets off rocks to bait their father's lines. The brother held his sister's hand, helping her climb over the rough outcroppings. On the way home he took the baskets and gave her a head start, letting her race before him down a smooth stretch of sand. Then he was running, too, and when he ran too far ahead he heard his little sister's voice calling his name, "Kerel, Kerel!" like the high, clear call of a bird.

Soon Kerel began fishing each day with their father, and Mikki was left alone to gather shellfish and bait their father's lines. Each afternoon she met the village boats as they pulled into harbor, and helped her father and brother bring in their catch.

She was happy, despite early loss. She had friends; she had her brother. She still had her father, a lean, hard-working man of few words. He was somber and distant, but there were times that his eyes softened when he looked at his children. There were times that the sadness in his face cleared. Occasionally he dropped words of praise—for Kerel's handling of the boat, for Mikki's fish stew—and then his children glowed with pride.

Gull's last feather-charm had long since frayed to pieces. It was Mikki's charms that Kerel and Father now wore.

Perhaps Mikki was careless. She didn't wash the gull feathers thoroughly enough. She didn't take care to promptly replace worn feathers. Perhaps it was that she simply didn't have her mother's touch. She made the types of charms that other women in the village made: simple necklaces of feathers and beads tied on bands of leather. They weren't Gull's designs, and never would be.

One day Mikki was spreading out seaweed to dry in the sun when she became aware of a sudden stillness. The air felt tight; no birds sang, nothing called nor moved. The drying rack fell from her fingers and she looked out to sea, her heart pounding. She saw dark clouds on the horizon, and a brilliant, eerie light flooding beneath.

She ran to the harbor. Other women and girls were already gathered there. The world held its breath. She saw the first fishing boats racing home, flying before a wall of light and the black storm-clouds massed above.

Wind rose off the sea. A spray of salt hit her eyes. She stood on the pier, waiting. And then the world went dark, sudden as the clap of a hand. Rain poured down in sheets, and waves swelled and whipped the bay into foam.

The first boats struggled in. Voices shouted, barely audible above the surging wind and surf. Women held shielded lanterns aloft in the gloom. Lines of rope were tossed and eager arms pulled the fishermen ashore. None of them were Mikki's father or crew; her father's boat wasn't there.

Straining, Mikki glimpsed a boat out past the harbor. She saw it sail by the rocks near the harbor entrance; she saw it making its way to safety and home. And then a sudden wave overtook it from behind; she saw the boat capsize.

Her scream joined the screams of the crowd, thin above the wind and sea.

She saw a second boat try for the harbor, and saw it dashed upon rocks.

She waited and waited, frozen and numb, but she never saw her father's boat at all.

***

It was the gods' blessing or whim that Kerel was not on his father's boat that day. Father's crew had taken another man on board in Kerel's stead, a crew member's cousin whose own boat was undergoing repairs and who needed to feed his family. The crew agreed to let the man fish with them that day, and to divide their catch with him.

And so Mikki still had her brother, though all else was lost.

At some point during that dreadful day, she became aware of Kerel standing beside her. He had returned from the river-town several miles inland, where he had gone to buy goods and run errands.

It was still raining, the sky dark as night. In the lantern-light Mikki saw the pale faces around her; she saw the wife and young sons of the fisherman who had taken Kerel's place. She could feel her brother crying next to her. She reached out, and they took and held each other's hands.

This is what we say in these coastal towns haunted by dreams of the Sea Witch: a finger bone is enough. A joint of a pinkie, a single knucklebone, the smallest scrap of flesh—these are enough to save a soul from the Sea Witch's halls, to call a soul home to rest. Take what you can, whatever you can save from the sea. Wash the remains in fresh water. Bind it in white cloth. Sing to it. You'll have to stay up a full night, singing the soul home. In the morning, rise and carry your loved one on a bier of fresh-cut wood. Carry him or her to high ground untouched by the sea. Bury your loved one, and scatter the grave with flowers.

For days after the storm, Mikki and Kerel wandered the shore, searching for their father's remains. They were joined by others looking for their own fathers or sons, husbands or brothers. Up and down the coast, fishing boats had been lost. Wreckage and bodies washed in over days. A few men from their village were retrieved—two men from the Gannet, one from the Wild Rose. But no one from the White Gull—-not a trace of Father or any of his crew.

***

Mikki lit candles for the soul of her father and the souls of the village's lost men and boys. She prayed to the Goddess of Mercy for them. On the family altar she set out a bowl of her father's favorite stew and the barley-cakes he had loved.

She went to her mother's grave and asked for Gull's intercession. She prayed that her mother's spirit might petition and win release of Father's soul from the ocean deeps. Around her, other women and girls were kneeling in their own family burial plots, making similar prayers. White flags fluttered in the field, marking the souls of those unburied, and signaling them home from the sea.

Kerel went to his mother's grave with Mikki. He knelt with her, his eyes red, but his prayers were silent.

***

It was a hard autumn. Three boats and a dozen men lost from the village. Nine men whose bodies were never retrieved. Survivors shared what they could with the widowed and orphaned. Kerel went fishing when he could with other boats in the village, and on boats from other ports. He found odd jobs, and Mikki took in extra work mending nets and baiting lines.

Winter came, cold and stormy. The fishing fleet was grounded. Mikki stretched the salt-fish-and-porridge with water until the grains could scarcely be seen. Her head spun from hunger.

In the spring, Kerel found steady work on a boat that launched from a port-town to the south. He rose each morning an hour before dawn and returned after the sun had set. Mikki combed the beach each day for the finest, whitest feathers she could find. She spent precious money on beads and on fine leather ties. She wove her charms, praying to Gull that this time she would get them right.

The air softened with warmth. The trees were in full leaf, the fields abloom with tiny bright flowers. Birds were nesting on the cliffs. Now the sun shone even after Kerel walked in the door after a full day's fishing. He whistled, and began speaking of plans to invest in a new boat with friends. Mikki's hand went to her heart as she thought of the crew he had lost. Kerel carefully pretended not to see.

Each evening, she put a few bites of supper aside for the family altar, for her father's soul. She wondered if he could taste it beneath the waves.

Spring slipped into summer and then into fall. Kerel told

Mikki that he meant to set sail on a merchant ship to southern seas.

"Six weeks down the coast to Ibrin," he said. "We'll unload and take on new cargo, continue down to the point and then sail east to the Thressian Islands. We'll avoid the winter storms here and ride the westward winds back. Three months in all, but Mikki, it's better than kicking my feet at the fire through another winter if the season here is poor. I'll make enough money for the payments on my share of a new boat this spring."

Mikki stood still, her dark eyes wide.

Kerel's own dark eyes pled with hers. "We've saved and I borrowed an advance on the pay," he said. "Enough for you to be comfortable. Our aunt and uncle will keep an eye out for you."

Mikki's cheeks burned as she realized that her brother had already made up his mind, had already laid out his plans.

"I...I told Jacil," Kerel hesitated. "I know that you don't like it that I told him first, but he's promised to watch out for you." Jacil was one of Kerel's friends. A nice boy.

"You like Jacil, don't you?" Kerel's tone was light. She knew what he was asking.

She thought of a boy who had sailed on Father's crew. Kerel's dearest friend. He had had freckles and beautiful hands, and a quick smile that flashed like lightning. She had never spoken of her feelings for him. She knew that Kerel mourned him at least as much as he mourned their father.

"Yes," Mikki said aloud. "I like Jacil well enough."

***

It's not only the souls of the drowned whom the Sea Witch calls. Sometimes, she calls to those still on land. A child on the beach goes missing. A young woman goes for a walk on the cliffs and never returns. An old fisherman disappears from his bed in the night.

Usually, there are signs. Usually, it's someone bereaved. Every village has its tale. A widow or heart-broken lover; a bereft parent. A seaman who escaped a wreck, but saw his captain washed overboard and his friends drowned before his eyes. Such a person's own eyes may turn empty, unseeing. He doesn't respond to his name; he doesn't see the sunlit world. His soul is trapped underwater, wandering the ocean floor.

If you can see the signs, you can perhaps keep the body safe until the soul returns. You can keep watch, keep vigil. A family will string feathers over the doorway along with branches and sprays from a rowan tree. Family members will feed the afflicted tea with bitter herbs. Sweet-leaf will be burned on the fire.

If there are no warning signs, there is nothing to be done. A girl vanishes, called down to the ocean depths. A boy jumps suddenly from cliff or boat or pier. Afterward, the village will whisper of missed signs, of the Sea Witch's irresistible song. Mothers will continue to comb the shore, searching for a scrap of bone to bury.

***

Mikki went to the docks of the southern port-town to see her brother off. Other family and friends accompanied them. As he went to hug her, she handed him a pouch. "Ten feather-charms inside," she said. "Each time a feather frays, take it off and put a new charm on. Promise me."

He smiled. "They don't wear out that quickly, Mikki. I won't be gone that long."

"You don't know how long you'll be gone." She tried to keep the tremor from her voice. "When you discard a charm, throw it into the sea. Maybe—maybe it will find its way to someone. Someone who could use it. They're weighted with beads of stone."

He held the pouch to his heart. He made as though to speak, and then stopped. His expression was unreadable. He hugged her tight, and said only, "I will."

***

Another hard winter. Wind and rain and the seas churned white with foam. Thunder and crashing waves a nightly lullaby. Mikki's cottage roof leaked and the walls shook in the wind. The cold seeped in like a relentless tide.

The fishermen were stranded on shore by the weather, adrift and grumbling. Mikki saw children hollow-eyed with hunger. Kerel had spoken truly: there was money enough for her to eat, and so she went from house to house sharing her barley-cakes and bread.

Mixed in with the scream and whine of the wind, mixed in with the crash and murmur of waves, Mikki sometimes thought she heard other notes. A chime of bells. A female voice. Something that was almost a song. She shivered and prayed and built up her fire.

She heard word of a fishing boat lost from a village to the north. A crew of brothers and cousins. They had set forth during a break in the weather, betting on fair skies for a chance at whitefish and silveroils. She didn't know their names.

"He's safer on that merchant ship than we are on our own boats here, Mikki," Jacil said. True to his word, Kerel's friend stopped by nearly every day. He was a comforting presence, cheerful and solidly built. He had fixed the leak in her roof, although it seemed scarcely warmer than before. He held his hands to her fire now. "Calm southern seas and one of the finest boats to launch from the shipyards of Ibrin…"

Mikki looked at her brother's friend, at his kind, broad face. She tried to smile.

Encouraged, Jacil kept on. "You were there, you saw the Kittiwake set sail. Biggest ship I've ever seen. Those merchant vessels are made to carry on through storms; they can ride waves half the height of our cliffs. And the captain—nothing but good words about him from everyone I've heard. A good captain. A good crew."

"A good crew," Mikki echoed. She imagined her brother on the open sea, riding waves half the height of the cliffs that flanked their village.

"He might even be on his way back now," Jacil said. "Another month, a month and a half. Kerel will be home soon."

***

A month. A month and a half. Mikki counted off the weeks in her head.

A ship from the Thressian Islands sailed into the port-town to the south. But it was not Kerel's ship, not The Kittiwake, and the crew had no knowledge of The Kittiwake's fortunes.

Another month. And then one more. Finally word from the merchants' guild: The Kittiwake had landed in the Thressian Islands on schedule at the beginning of winter, taking on cargo there as planned. It had been seen departing for the westward journey back. But where was it now?

Anchored in a warm southern isle, Jacil said. Blown off course or damaged in a storm, but under repairs and soon to make its way back.

Somewhere on the coast south of Ibrin, Mikki's aunt said. Delayed, but already on course again.

Lost in wild seas, others whispered darkly. Blown far off course and drifting under strange stars. Caught in a whirlpool that circulates endlessly, forever, near the bottom of the world. Caught in the tentacles of a beast whose face is sand and rock at the bottom of the sea.

Gone, Mikki's heart told her. Torn apart by storms. Swamped and capsized like the fishing boat she had seen last year. Broken on rocks like the second boat she had seen destroyed. Vanished, like her father's boat and like so many other boats from the coast.

"Don't," Jacil said, watching as Mikki lit a second candle on her family altar. "It's too soon, Mikki; you haven't waited long enough. Ships are delayed all the time. Did you hear of the Plover? It sailed into Ibrin Bay half a year late."

Mikki stared at the flame she had lit. Her dark eyes were haunted, but her voice was calm.

"How cold do you think it is," she said, "at the bottom of the sea?"

Jacil hesitated. "Mikki," he said finally. "It might be different in the southern seas. The stories they tell. . . I know I've laughed at some of them. But they believe different things there. Different gods and spirits. Maybe. . . . maybe it's not the same when a man drowns in southern seas."

Mikki thought of the Sea Witch. She thought of the songs she heard in the night, the voice calling and the chime of drowned bells.

"It's all one sea," she said.

***

This is the story we tell on our coast: the souls of the drowned are trapped in the Sea Witch's halls. As long as their bodies lie in her realm, there can be no release.

But it's a story that some—that most—have always resisted. Children light candles on altars and pray. White flags are planted to call spirits home. Ancestral ghosts are petitioned. There is hope against hope that fate can be changed.

Mikki ran to the top of the cliffs and threw her feather-charms into the sea. She watched them spin through the air—half-made things, unfinished, some of them completed but torn apart by her own hands that day. Why had she spent the winter tying them? Why had she combed the shore for the perfect white plume? Her frail charms had never done anything. They could never hold back the might of the sea.

She watched her charms tumble and fall. She saw them caught by the slate-gray waves.

She had prayed to her mother's spirit, the mother she could not remember. The only family member buried in the safe black earth. Gull had never protected anyone. She had not even protected herself.

Mikki watched the last of her charms sink out of sight. Seagulls flew beneath her, banking and soaring into the wind.

***

That night she went to her aunt and uncle's home for dinner. Her young cousins chattered and laughed and passed the bread, and afterward the family asked her to stay the night. There was no room, and yet on another night she might have accepted. There had been times during the lonely winter when she had curled on the floor before her aunt's fire alongside her youngest cousins, grateful to feel their sleeping bodies beside her, to hear the breath of another person. She knew that her kin worried about her. But this night she thanked them and turned away.

She went home to her own cold house. She sat before her own empty hearth, her eyes unseeing.

"Will you marry him?" her aunt had asked. Jacil had proposed to her that morning. Mikki had not given anyone a reply.

Of course you will, a voice inside her said now. Jacil would care for her. He was a good man. And she was a girl alone in the world, brotherless and fatherless. She could grow to love him. She thought of what Kerel would have wanted.

She thought of Kerel at the bottom of the sea.

She heard the Sea Witch's song again, chiming faintly beneath the wind. A song like a flute, and then like the piercing cry of a gull. A woman's voice, singing a song she knew, a lullaby she had once heard. . . Light flashed in her memory, she felt cool hands; a curtain of dark, silken hair brushed her cheek. She was a child, lying feverish in bed, and her mother was singing to her. She struggled to get up, telling herself This isn't real, and she heard another voice, her brother's voice, calling to her frightened and far away, Mikki, Mikki. . . She heard other voices, fainter still. The voices of all lost beneath the waves. She felt a feather in her hand, and she knew that it was the beautiful, perfect feather she had always sought.

She opened her eyes. The feather was real.

She traced the long feather shaft with a trembling hand. She felt the edges: smooth and strong. It was whiter than foam, white as the rare snow that sometimes fell on the coast; it glowed, and there was not a speck of dirt or color to be seen.

She heard her mother's voice, and knew that this time it was true.

She closed her eyes, held tight to her feather, and let the Sea Witch's song take her away.

* * *

She was a little brown fish in the great ocean. A fish so small, so inconsequential, that she had no name; fishermen would not waste their breath on her. She swam through the holes of fishermen's nets; she swam past their lines, beneath their boats; she swam downward, down, and all sunlight slipped away.

She was one of hundreds of tiny, nameless brown fish. They swam in the cold depths, moving past one another without notice. The only light came from the tiny flames, like candle lights, that the other fish held in their mouths.

There were walls of stone, black and shimmering. There were forests of kelp. There was a woman on a throne, and her green hair drifted and swirled in the tides. Her face shone like a pale moon. Her lovely eyes shifted from green to gray to blue to green again. She lifted one hand languidly, gracefully, and at her signal a small school of fish came and circled above her head, the candle lights in their mouths making a living, glowing crown.

The newest little fish, just come from the sea-surface, swam forward to join them. She, too, was a servant of the Sea Witch.

***

She had served the Sea Witch for untold eons. She had served the Sea Witch all her life, and all past lives she might have had. She knew nothing else. There was nothing else to know.

She swam the great ocean looking for drowned souls to bring back to the Sea Witch's halls. She swam through great wrecks, ships near the size of palaces; she swam through rusting black cannons and broken chains. She found some souls still drifting near their bodies, confused. Other souls had already been washed far from their remains, whole crews scattered across the sea.

The souls were little lights floating in the deeps. Tiny golden lights—the sight stirred some memory within her. Whenever she came across a soul, she took it into her mouth and swam back with it to the Sea Witch's halls. In those silent halls, shelves stretched endlessly along the black stone walls. The little fish would deposit the soul carefully upon a shelf, there to join an endless line of souls shining steadily at the bottom of the sea.

The Sea Witch sat amidst this all, watching the lights increase around her. Her eyes flickered with the colors of the ocean surface. Sometimes, her eyes looked sad.

***

Sometimes, a soul would try to speak.

They would whisper as the little fish took them into her mouth. They would murmur snatches of their memories; they would plead with her for a glimpse of the sun, a breath of air. She did not understand their words. She carried them with her, deep and deeper still, until at last their voices faltered. They were silent as she placed them on the waiting shelves.

She knew the valleys and hills of the ocean floor; she knew the wide plateaus, the vents of fire, the canyons and trenches and undersea mountains. She knew all manner of human ships and boats. She saw remnants of human life spilled from the wrecks: cracked plates and cups, a shaving blade, a woman's comb. A child's doll, the porcelain head broken open, the silken hair rotted away. She saw all manner of corpses and bones, and the talismans that many wore or left behind. Figures of gods and spirits, carved in wood and gold and ivory and jade, hung from chains of silver or gold. Amulets stuffed with dried flower petals; vials of blessed, black dirt. Lockets with loved ones' pictures. Lockets that held pieces of parchment, inscribed with prayers and spells.

She saw a charm of feathers twisted around the neck of a freshly drowned corpse. The soul still floated nearby, bobbing in gentle currents. She stared at the decaying feathers, and something stirred within.

***

Ten feather-charms. She had given ten charms to someone, a long time ago. Charms weighted with beads of stone. Each charm woven for a face she could no longer picture.

She found the first one tangled on a coral branch in tropical seas. The beads glinted; the leather bands were still supple and strong. The feathers looked as fresh as the day she'd tied them, but shone white-hot like pieces of the sun. Caught in the charm's loops was a single glowing soul.

The little fish bit and pulled at the charm, at the tangle of feathers and soul. The soul whispered, and she felt it break free and slide inside her. She knew her name. She remembered everything.

"Kerel," she said.

"Mikki," he replied.

The feathers slid off the leather ties, one by one. She felt them cling to her, melt into her scales. They flared, and she was an explosion of light. Then they dimmed, and they were merely ordinary brown scales, a part of her like the rest of her skin.

She began laughing shakily, giddily. "You're so far from home," she told her brother, and he wept because so was she.

It was easier to find the others, then. She heard them calling to her across the sea. They had all drowned off the same coast, within a few miles of one another, yet their bones had been tumbled far and their souls even farther. She could hear their voices clearly now; she understood their words. Kerel knew them, too, and he helped her find the souls of the men from their village, all who had drowned in the storm that wrecked their father's ship.

Hathir, solid as an oak tree, and gentle and kind. He had been like a second uncle to her.

Feren, thin as a grass-blade, who quipped and laughed at his own jokes.

Karsen, who whittled spinning tops and toys for the village children every New Year's celebration. Athel, barely more than a boy, who used to flick her pigtails when they were children. Farsil and Kiernan and Relis...

She found them held in glowing feather-charms, entangled in seaweed and coral, caught on the rotting mast of a ship or the edge of a rock. Anchored and waiting for her. She took them into her mouth, and she took the feathers for new scales.

"You can't hold us all," Kerel warned, and it was true. They were too many, too heavy and bright. They burned her cheeks, her teeth.

"Hide us," they whispered, and she unwound a feather-charm and used it to tie them all together to the corner of a jagged rock. She tucked them into a rock fissure.

Kerel she did not release. She had swallowed him, and he stayed within her, lodged beneath her heart.

Five left. Four. Three. Two.

She found him, the freckled boy with the brilliant smile. The one she might have loved, had they had more time.

"I saw him," said the soul who had once had beautiful eyes. "He was with me; he tried to save me. And then we drowned, and a brown fish took him away."

And Mikki and Kerel knew where the last soul, their father, had gone.

***

She swam back over the great ocean plains; she swam over the undersea mountain ranges, the valleys and trenches and vents of flame. She returned to the Sea Witch's shimmering black halls.

She looked at the shelves and shelves of souls and despaired.

None of these souls spoke. None called out to her. There were no shining white feathers coiled around her father—nothing to mark him from the rest. He had been taken before a charm could find him and hold him fast.

"Where do I begin?" she whispered. And Kerel within whispered, "At the beginning."

They moved down the endless rows, the golden lights burning steadily around them. Servants of the Sea Witch came and went, adding new souls to the shelves. All ignored Mikki.

She called out, and the vast silence drowned her voice. No one replied.

"He never did talk much," Kerel said.

She laughed weakly. But a pang hit her fish-heart as she thought of how little she'd known him, her quiet, grieving father. She'd thought that maybe he talked more with Kerel, that Kerel surely knew him better, for they had gone out to sea together each day…

Mikki and Kerel went on. On and on. Ever closer to the heart of the Sea Witch's labyrinth of halls. They saw her at times, walking in the distance, her hair drifting luminously behind her.

How much time had passed? How long would the Sea Witch let Mikki roam these halls?

Days later, years later, an unknown immensity of time. . . Kerel froze within her and said, "Mikki. Here."

She stopped. The little lights burned before her, each one exactly the same.

"Here," Kerel said again, although his voice was uncertain. "Somewhere here, one of them, I can feel it…" She swam in a slow circle. Kerel inside tensed with frustration. "No, not that one, not that one, but close by, I know it…" Loss echoed in his voice. Loss that did not begin on a single storm-wracked day, but that stretched out from the years before.

"If we had a feather-charm," Mikki said. "Something to call him, something to catch him. . ."

Kerel was still. When he finally spoke again, his voice was strange. "Mikki, I can feel a feather inside you. A feather in your heart."

It was as though the cold ocean had vanished. She remembered sitting alone in a dry room. She remembered holding a beautiful, perfect white feather in her hand. The feather her mother had given her.

"Take the feather out," Mikki told her brother.

He pulled it from her heart, pushed it up her gullet and helped her hold it in her teeth so that it could shine to the outer world. She swam slowly before the shelves of souls, the feather incandescent in her mouth.

She saw the Sea Witch enter the far end of the hall.

Now souls were waking and stirring all around. Their voices were like the rustling of leaves in the sunlit world. They were calling out to her, to the shining feather she held.

Mikki saw the Sea Witch draw near. At the other end of the hall, a school of fish turned and began to swim toward the feather's white light.

Kerel gasped as the Sea Witch's face came clearly into view. Mikki knew that he saw it, too—the fine bones of her pale face, the graceful curve of her eyes. The Sea Witch resembled their mother.

The feather blazed in her mouth; she was blinded by it. But she heard a voice, familiar, quietly speaking her name. She swam to it, unseeing. She felt a soul push up against her feather and make its way through the barbs, into the quill. The light increased still more; it was intolerable. The soul moved up the quill, and the light flared through her; her bones hummed. And then the light dimmed, and she knew the feather was a part of her again, a feather-scale like the rest. Her father was within her. "Mikki," he said softly. And then, "Kerel."

Fish eyes cannot cry. But she felt something in her contract, and then loosen and ease. She felt her father settle in next to Kerel. She held the two of them now, her family. Two golden lights nestled beneath her heart.

The feather from her mother had dimmed, but it did not go out. It shone still in the darkness. All her feather-scales shone. She was a white light, a beacon. Souls around her cried out.

A feather-charm flashed above. A string of feathers holding eight souls, men and boys from her village. Lost crew of the Gannet, Sweet Rose, and her father's boat, White Gull.

She swallowed them all, taking them within her. The last feathers became her last white scales. And the souls were not heavy, as they had been before. They were light itself. They were sails full of wind; they were lanterns of hot air, pulling her upward.

She began to rise.

She heard the souls on their shelves calling for her. Take us! Take us with you! they cried. She gulped souls down as she floated past. They slid in, and told her of their pasts. A slave thrown from a ship for disobedience. A sailor whose foot slipped on a wet deck. A girl who drowned herself from grief.

She was rising toward the ocean surface. She was buoyant with souls.

"You can't take them all," Kerel whispered as she rose faster and faster.

And another voice, a new one, said, No. You can't take them all. But you can take all you can. It might have been her mother's voice. It might have been her own.

Far below, the Sea Witch stood and watched. Her green-grey eyes were expressionless. Her hair and dress billowed in invisible currents, and her servants watched silently with her.

But Mikki was looking upward. The surface was rushing toward her. She saw the light growing stronger and clearer. She remembered the sunlit world, the life she had lived there. She had time to mourn it, to mourn what might have been. To grieve the life she might have chosen: marriage to Jacil, children with him, an ordinary life in the village with living family and friends.

The surface rushed ever nearer. Her scales had turned to feathers. She thought she saw the sky. And then her last thoughts disappeared. She was flying upward, and there was no separation between water and air. She was melting into the light, she and her father and brother and all the souls she could carry with her wings.

***

But our story does not end here. Not quite.

You might understand it now, that wooden fish charm you hold. The little shrines you may have seen along the shore, at the foot of a pier. Shrines to the fish-bird, the bird-fish. Prayers to both the White Gull and Brown Fish.

No? Then let me explain. It is said that Mikki did not stay in the Realms of Light. It is said that she went back for the souls she could not save. She scours the oceans even now; she enters the Sea Witch's halls and takes souls from the very shelves. The Sea Witch merely goes about her ancient business, collecting drowned souls; and Mikki goes about her business in turn—Mikki the Light-Bringer, Soul-Savior, the Winged Fish.

Did you keep count during the tale? Ten charms she gave Kerel: one so that he would always have a charm to wear, and nine to be tossed to the sea. But the tenth charm never found their father. Perhaps it found a different soul to save; perhaps Mikki has already used it, rescued that soul and taken the feathers. Or perhaps this is what she uses over and over, this single charm, saving lost souls one at a time.

And the Sea Witch in her black halls: perhaps she is merely holding the souls in place for Mikki, keeping them safe on her shelves. Perhaps that has always been her ancient task. Is that why she sings from the sea?

This is a story we tell each other, here on our lovely, perilous coast. Here, where storms blow and bells chime in the deep, and we pray and light candles in the dark.

LESSER IS MORE

Sandi Leibowitz

Sandi Leibowitz is a native New Yorker who writes speculative fiction and poetry, mostly based on fairy-tales, myth and folklore. Her works appear in such places as Goblin Fruit, Mythic Delirium, Niteblade, The Golden Key, Apex and Strange Horizons. One of her poems is forthcoming in Best Horror of the Year, Vol. 5, edited by Ellen Datlow.

In 1841, I was thirty-two years old, working in New York City as a journalist for the *Daily Chronicle*. At nights, I scribbled under the aegis of my own muse, publishing the occasional story or poem with a modicum of success. Edmund Lesser also lived in town, though we'd never run into each other.

We'd been best friends as boys at Barston's Academy for Young Gentlemen until his adoptive father, John Lesser, had forbidden him to become a writer; after that, we no longer had anything in common. By chance we both went to the University of Virginia where I learned that John Lesser had disinherited Edmund—cut him off without a penny. He'd been forced to leave the university, for Lesser had never paid the bills. Edmund, who changed his name back to Perry, had enlisted in the army. Years later, I was pleased to hear he also lived in New York and had been hired as editor of *The Town Crier*, a new magazine that had received many favorable reviews, though I had not yet subscribed to it.

One day, an envelope arrived at my office. It contained a scribbled note in unfamiliar handwriting shaky as an old man's. It was signed by Edmund Perry, requesting that I visit him on Chatham Street. It surprised me that the editor of *The Town Crier* should live at so unsavory an address. But I was curious to see him and learn how he had managed such success after the terrible treatment he'd received from his stepfather. I sent a messenger with my acceptance. I would visit him at the end of my day's work.

Chatham Street was even grimmer than I'd pictured it, every other storefront a tavern or a dance hall. The streets were not illuminated by the new gas lamps. I imagined a robber lurking in every shadow. My trepidation increased as I approached No. 113, the only door to which opened onto yet another tavern. Obscured by a haze of smoke, solitary men hunkered over their whiskeys and gins, while small groups of the semi-inebriated (and not so semi) shared crude jokes.

"Mr. Perry's rooms?" I asked the surly bartender.

"Number Five." He nodded to a set of stairs at the back. I climbed upward, praying the rickety banister would hold and the rotting wood not collapse beneath my feet.

I knocked upon the door marked 5. I heard a shuffle and the scrape of a chair.

"Who—who is there?" came a harried whisper.

"It is I—Harry Stratham. Edmund?"

The door was unlatched but a chain prevented it from opening fully. A haggard face peeked out.

"Harry! Come in. Quickly!"

Edmund opened the door just widely enough for me to squeeze through, and immediately locked it.

He sported a dark moustache, which might have given him a dapper air had the rest of his countenance not been so gravely compromised. Purple bags shadowed his eyes and the left one sagged. Grey streaked his handsome black hair, now thinned. His figure was gaunt, no longer that of the athletic hero of Barston's. The celebrated editor of *The Town Crier*, prematurely aged, looked haunted.

"Oh, Harry it's so good to see you!" A nervous smile spread across those sallow features as he swept a pile of manuscripts from a chair to make room for me. "Sit, sit. Will you join me in a brandy?"

We discussed the vagaries of our careers. Not all of Edmund's works had met with success. I took the bull by the horns.

"I read the review of your Tamerlane in the *Manhattan Review*. Damned unfair, I must say."

"You read it?"

"The poem? Of course. That Drawley! He has nothing better to do than spew his vitriolic attacks against better writers. He's treated Irving and Dickens just as badly. You mustn't take it to heart. People only read him to see how vicious he can get."

Perry tilted back his chair and laughed heartily. "Don't condemn him. I wrote the review, too."

"You—what?"

"I wrote Samuel Drawley's review of Edmund Perry's *Tamerlane*. Best publicity I've ever gotten. Drawley really helps pay the bills. Remember, I don't have an inheritance to rely on. Stories in magazines, the occasional book of poems, and the editorship of *The Town Crier* give me barely enough to live on. Drawley's vile reviews are very popular. Without him, I couldn't afford my guests a proper glass of brandy." He lifted his glass in salute.

I couldn't help remembering the last time we drank together, just before he left the university, when he'd been reduced to such poverty he didn't even own a glass. I was sure he remembered it as well.

"Do you follow Worthley's column in *The Tattler*?" He picked up a folded copy from his desk.

I nodded. Suddenly, I realized why the name had always seemed familiar. When we were still at Barston's Edmund had gotten around Lesser's proscription against writing by using a number of different pseudonyms. Jonathan Worthley was one of them. "Not you, too?"

"The same. Worthley's been a good champion of my poetry. I was most grateful for his defense of my *Tamerlane*. His opinions rarely coincide with those of Drawley." His eyebrows quirked up. I must have imagined that the bags under his eyes had vanished. "There are others, too." He pointed to neat piles of papers on his desk. Could each one really represent a different pseudonym?

A knock came at the door.

Edmund started. A look of fear swallowed up his bonhomie.

"Harry, will you—would you—answer it for me?" he pleaded, as if asking me to dispatch a venomous serpent.

"Of course." I rose. He placed a hand on my shoulder to stay me.

"Use the chain. Don't let him in."

I did as he asked.

"Is this the abode of Eddie Dessavoo?" asked a young man who shifted from foot to foot.

Before I could answer, Edmund called out, "Edouard Desavoue no longer lives here. He did, but he's gone."

"I have a bill from Markham's," the young man insisted. "Dessavoo owes Markham's thirty dollars and 43 cents. I've been sent to collect."

Rather than appearing distressed, Edmund seemed relieved. "I don't know where he's disappeared to," he called out. "No forwarding address. You must seek him elsewhere."

I apologized to the messenger, who reluctantly departed, and shut the door. Edmund jumped up to lock it.

"Does this happen often? Who is this Desavoue?"

Edmund laughed nervously. "I am." He drained his glass

and promptly poured himself another. "Desavoue became necessary when I fell behind on some bills. I attempted to start my own magazine and needed capital. My major subscribers pulled out at the last minute. Desavoue wrote a series of articles on the plight of struggling new publications in America."

I laughed, meaning to congratulate him on his successful ploy, the daring of the fox eluding the hounds. But Edmund's haunted look returned.

"That's why I've asked you here," he whispered. He glanced about the room as if the walls conspired against him. "I trust you, Harry. You've never stabbed me in the back or disappointed me. Never made a promise you didn't keep."

I felt a hot flush of shame, remembering how little I'd done for him when he'd lost his inheritance and all semblance of family. Ah. Desavoue—French for "disinherited."

"You can count on me, Edmund," I said, and meant it.

"It is about these—others—that I mean to speak to you." He licked his lips, gathering his thoughts, or his courage.

"When I was a boy—Edmund Lesser—I wondered about Edmund Perry, what he might have been like. What if my father had not…disappeared? What if my mother had lived? What if I'd grown up knowing her and my brother David? I would have taken to the stage like my parents…I think I would have liked that."

"You would have flourished there," I assured him.

"I wondered just how differently I would have turned out. Happier, surely. I would have known a mother's love. Fanny Lesser was distant, lukewarm in her affections. She and my stepfather went away to England for a year when I was seven, did you know? Left me behind with the servants. Lesser never sent a single letter. Fanny just wrote now and then, reminding me to be a good boy, occasionally sending her love. It's a very different thing to be *sent* love, than to have it *given* you, I think.

"Even without a mother and a brother—a brother! If only I'd gotten to know him.! If only my uncle had taken me in… As a boy, I often daydreamed about these alternate lives. So it was always easy for me to create these…others. My imagination never falters. I just pick a name, a profession, a personality.

"As I've grown older, these…*others*…have come in handy. When I enlisted, I created Harrison Ellmore to put everything of Edmund *Lesser* behind me." He spat at the name of his detested once-benefactor. "But it turned out fortuitous that I created this new identity. Things started out well for me in the army, but…I ran into some trouble. I received a dishonorable discharge. I'm glad Edmund Perry's name needn't be attached to that shameful chapter.

"Some of it was a game. I loved to create new *noms de plume*. On any given day there might be six pieces by me published in different magazines or newspapers. They were all mine, and no one knew. It was my secret triumph. In print, veiled behind these names, I could glorify my work as Strasser in the *Republic*, while vilifying that of Le Rennet in the *Star-Eagle*. I enjoyed duping the reading public. When creditors came hounding me, as so often happened, fictive identities like Desavoue were useful.

"But Harry…" He put his hands to his brow and stopped.

"Whatever it is, Edmund, you can tell me."

He lifted his head. His eyes were wild. "You'll think me mad! Perhaps I am, perhaps I am," he muttered.

I wondered if that truly were the case.

"They're after me, Harry."

"Who are?"

His lips trembled.

"The...*Others*. They are real. And they've begun to clamor for their share of the money. But there isn't enough! I can barely live on it myself. I can't support them, I can't!" He flung his arms out in a passion.

"You saw. You *saw*. Desavoue has run up debts with his tailor—he likes to dress well. Worthley overspends on fine wines. You see what *I'm* reduced to drinking! Le Rennet is a womanizer. He buys jewels and...makes promises I can't keep! Strasser wishes to travel abroad."

My heart broke to hear his ravings.

"You do think me mad," he said at last.

"I...think you're under a strain. Edmund, you know you created these personae yourself. The newspaper bylines, the controversies the reviews stir up, the creditors using these names to harass you for payments, all these things lend an air of reality to their existence. You work incessantly, and for little pay. How much sleep do you get?"

He listened with an air of rational calm. "You're probably right," he said at last. "I beg of you, Harry, go to the offices of *The Town Crier*. Augustus Macklin, the publisher, is withholding my first payment. He refuses to send it by courier and I daren't leave this room, I daren't! They're waiting for me. They've been stalking me for weeks. Who knows what else they want from me besides money? Macklin will only give the cash to me in person, even if I send him the next installment—it's not as if I can't write my columns at home. You must go for me, Harry."

"But how will that help? He won't hand over your payment to me, either."

"No, but some of the Others will be watching and waiting for me there—at least one of them. You can deliver my column and ask Macklin if he'll give you my money. No harm in trying. But the important thing is…" he grabbed me by the lapels and drew my face right up against his, "I need you to go and see if *They* really are there, so I can know for certain whether or not I am indeed mad. If I am…I don't know what I shall do to help myself. And if they are really there—I don't know what to do about that either. I don't! But at least I'll know. I'll know." Perspiration beaded Edmund's forehead. His eyes glittered like a fever victim's.

I cursed John Lesser. It was his withdrawal of support, coupled with the ban on writing, that had led Edmund to create these fictive selves. Poverty and perpetual struggle had dogged the steps of a man educated as a gentleman, raised with a gentleman's expectations.

"I'll go, Edmund. In the meantime, try to rest."

"Thank you, Stratham. You're my only friend." When his hand grasped mine I felt it tremble.

The next morning, I set out early to execute Perry's request. A light snowfall had already dusted the streets and more was steadily falling. Snow always lends fairy-tale glamour to the New York streets—at least until the soot renders it a grimy grey. I turned down Nassau Street, where most publishers were located, onto Cedar, through alleys that were rem-nants of the old Indian trails. I arrived at a row of tidy brick buildings. *The Town Crier's* headquarters were located up a flight of stairs well-lit by windows looking onto the street. Surely Edmund's fortune is on the rise, I thought, now that he's employed by such a thriving, if modest, company. His demented fancy is but a slight setback. I'll be able to set his mind at ease and all will be well.

A door with "Town Crier" painted in crisp black letters opened into a room containing five or six desks where earnest young men scribbled furiously or scanned lengthy galleys. When I announced my errand, one jumped up and rapped at the door to the publisher's office.

Augustus Macklin saw me immediately, cordially complimenting me on my work and encouraging me to submit to his magazine. He did not, however, release Edmund's monies, suggesting that he did so not because he did not trust me to deliver them but because, regrettably, he needed them to lure the wayward editor back to his post. I made my excuses for Edmund the best I could, hinting that he suffered from a contagious but nonetheless not life-threatening illness and thus could not show up in person. Macklin gave me a terse smile and coolly showed me out.

As I wended my way along Hyde Street toward my own office, I heard someone walking behind me. Unlike the major thoroughfares, thronged with carriages and pedestrians as the work day began, this small backstreet was otherwise deserted. I would shortly be passing by both Gowan's and Wiley and Putnam's. No reason why I should not check my notebook for titles of books on my list to purchase. I paused to rifle through the pages, though in truth my eyes did not focus on the list. The footsteps behind me stopped as well. When I moved forward, they started up again. I picked up my pace. So did my shadow.

As I stowed the notebook in my jacket pocket I purposefully dropped my pencil in the snow, giving myself a chance to glance behind. Someone indeed lurked there. Instead of pretending he wasn't on my trail, he gave me a wicked leer. I caught my breath. It was Edmund!

But no, this fellow was older, with a trim brown beard and prodigious side-whiskers. Edmund could not have afforded a pardessus with such luxuriant fur, nor one so well fitted. Yet it was Edmund's face! How could this be? I shivered at the thought of a supernatural explanation.

Then I realized: this must be his brother, whom he presumed off in Peru. Did David Perry believe Edmund to be Lesser's heir still? The thought that my friend's own brother should torture him in an effort to extort money, rather than offering him filial love and support, angered me.

"David Perry. What do you want of me?" I demanded.

The man sneered. "You are mistaken. Jonathan Worthley, at your service, sir." He doffed his silk topper and bowed.

"Cease this farce. Your brother has never done you any harm. Let him be!"

"I assure you, I have no brother, sir, no flesh and blood relations of any kind. I do not know of what you are speaking." The man pushed past me and exited onto Nassau Street.

I strode off in anger. It was only when I'd almost turned onto Nassau that I realized that the snowy pavement before me was as white and unsullied as a blank page. I looked back at the path I'd taken. Only the imprints of my own boots appeared in the white powder.

Throughout the day this odd event kept thrusting itself to my attentions. I was so taciturn and pale that my publisher, fearing I was ill, insisted I leave early. I gladly complied. But I did not head for my own apartments. I had to see Edmund.

Now that it was December, the evening gloom fell in early afternoon. Ordinarily the sight of the white flurries set aglow by the gas lamps put me in mind of sylphs and fairies. But this day I noticed instead the bat-like shadows they cast upon the ground. What would I tell Edmund? If I confirmed that the mysterious persons harassing him were not figments of his imagination, how would that help his mental stability? On the other hand, if I said I suspected his brother to be playing tricks on him, surely that would bring him no relief, either. But what of the lack of footprints in the snow?

I continued on my way to Chatham Street, arguing with myself about the possibilities. When I knocked at the door of Room No. 5, I heard murmuring and the sounds of movement.

"Edmund, it's me, Harry. Let me in."

The door unlocked. Perry peeked through the chain. "Come in, Stratham," he said in a strained voice.

As before, he locked the door the instant I pushed myself through. Unlike before, he remained behind me. And we were not alone in the room. Several men waited inside.

"At last. We've been waiting for you." Edmund's voice seemed strange.

I whirled around. It wasn't Edmund. It was the man who'd called himself Worthley.

I turned back to the men assembled. "Who are you?" I demanded.

They laughed, the tones ranging from tenor to bass. At exactly the same moment they stopped. The coincidence struck me as very odd.

"Why not introduce ourselves, gentlemen?" The speaker, dressed in a dove-grey suit in the latest Paris fashion, bowed with continental correctness."Henri Le Rennet."

"Samuel Drawley," said a portly fellow whose paunch strained against his waistcoat.

"Wilhelm Strasser." A lock of tawny hair fell across his fore-head. He swept it aside with a manicured hand.

A thin man with melancholy eyes and a guilty expression mumbled, "David Pemberton." At his utterance I recognized a fellow Bostonian.

"Harrison Ellmore," snarled a brawny, bearded man. Despite his receding hairline, he struck me as extremely strong and even more dangerous.

"Edouard Desavoue," drawled a fop in a fine suit with an oversized cravat in the new style.

I recognized all of these names: Edmund's *noms de plume*.

"Impossible. Those names were made up by my friend when he was a boy. He—"

Why had I not seen it before? Despite the differences in build, coloring and demeanor, each man bore a remarkable resemblance to Edmund Perry.

"Impossible!" I cried again, doubting my own sanity.

The men laughed—once more ending eerily at the same moment.

"Not impossible, as you see," said Desavoue.

"Your friend Mr. Perry was very gifted," Drawley remarked.

"W-was?" I sputtered.

In a fluid movement the men stepped aside, forming two groups that parted like stage curtains. If only the scene they revealed had been part of some cheap melodrama. On the floor lay a body, eyes bulging, a rope tightened round his neck as if he were a common criminal. Edmund Perry. He looked so small and vulnerable in his frayed suit.

"Which of you has done this dastardly deed?" I cried, kneeling beside the body in grief. "And why? Why?"

Le Rennet pulled closer. "We had to."

"Did he not create you? You owe your lives to him!"

"True," Worthley responded. "But we had only half-lives. We did not draw breath until our twenties."

"My life didn't begin till I was thirty-four," Drawley interrupted.

"He gave us no pasts. No families," Worthley continued.

"We went on to create our own lives, carve our presents," Strasser added. "But how can I live without a history? It's unnatural."

"He owed us," Ellmore growled. "He refused to give us what we wanted."

I had no doubt that this brute had been the one who had garroted Edmund.

"There was only one other way to achieve what we wanted," resumed Worthley, the apparent leader. "We had to kill Edmund Perry. Once he died, we would cease to be half-fiction and half-flesh. Our lives would become whole." He breathed deeply. A healthful flush suffused his face, as if a fasting man had just fed. "Already I feel my life fleshing out. I recall my sisters and brothers, my parents, my childhood in Albany."

Ellmore's jaw clenched. "Before I joined the army, I committed a string of robberies. And other crimes…" His face became even more savage, if that were possible.

Strasser wept into his hands. "I remember her now. Elena! Elena!" He uncovered his face. "Despite the tragedy of my life…my lost love…I still prefer this pain to the blank slate of my life before. I regret the loss of our creator," he looked pitying at the corpse of my friend, "but it was necessary."

"Your selfish desires cannot justify murder!" I cried.

Worthley strode over to me. I took an involuntary step backward. Ellmore positioned himself behind me, blocking my access to the door. "Why, Mr. Stratham, we need you. Now that we have full lives, we wish to live them fully."

"I shall return to New Orleans," Desavoue said. "I shall go home, now that I know where home is." He and the rest closed ranks, hemming me in.

"We cannot have the police dodging our steps," Pemberton said apologetically.

"Interfering with our futures now that we have pasts," Drawley said.

"What do you want of me? Just disappear. Go off to wherever the devil you wish to go."

"We have no desire to be hanged," Worthley said. "Yesterday I told you I had no brothers. But different though we are…" he nodded at the circle of men, the ones Edmund had called the Others, "in this cause we are all brethren. We would not sacrifice any one of our number to achieve our independence."

"We require a murderer," Ellmore said.

"Sorry, Stratham. You're the only one we can rely on." Worthley pinned back my arms. Ellmore grabbed the poker from the fireplace and aimed it at my head. I felt the blow and fell, unconscious, to the floor. When I awoke, the Others were gone.

I know my story strains credulity. You say the bartender has testified that no visitors except myself climbed the stairs to Mr. Perry's room. I well believe it. The Others are not ordinary men of flesh and blood like you and me. I had no reason to murder my dear friend. You must believe me. You must! I swear that everything I've told you is true .

FARGONE

J.S. Veter

Jessica's work had been published in New Realm Magazine, Beneath Ceaseless Skies, and by Seventh Star Press. Her novel 'Gateway' came out in 2012. 'Six' was published in 2016.

Kush Apbuscan would never forgive Ambarr Ping for marrying his sister.

They had been friends for forty long cycles. Their friendship had lasted through school, through puberty, and even through that time Kush had dyed Ambarr's genital prong bright yellow.

In fairness to Kush, he had been very drunk when he'd found the yellow dye, and Ambarr had not been awake to protest.

In spite of their long friendship, however, and in spite of the obvious love Kush's sister had for Ambarr, Kush promised himself on the day of the wedding that he would never speak to Ambarr again.

This made life difficult for all three of them.

It is hard enough to avoid family when living in a good-sized town. In a large city, it can sometimes feel as if the people you want to avoid have moved in next door. But when you live and work in the ass-end of the Hupt Galactic Expanse, on Fargone Station, at the dead-end of level 6, blue section, there is no chance of avoiding anyone. And ever since the Virtual Cinema had closed down, business had dropped to practically nothing. So what was there to do day after day but drink chai and visit with the neighbours? And what was there to do when the one thing there was to do was the one thing you'd sworn never to do again?

Which was pretty much what Cara, the aforementioned

sister, wondered one morning as she looked out the front window of the shop she shared with Ambarr, into the front window of Kush's shop, which was directly across the Via.

What was Kush doing?

Not three minutes ago, four Hupt officers had shown up, bristling with armour and weaponry. One after another, they had trooped into Kush's shop. Surely they were not there to buy boots.

"Hoi, Gimgim!" Cara called, pushing aside the beaded curtain hanging over her doorway. The chai seller changed direction, pushing his cart ahead of him.

"Cara-mai," he said, dipping to the side respectfully. "The usual?"

"Naa, Gimgim, it's too early for me," Cara said. "But do you know what our Kush is up to? There's four Hupti in there even now."

Gimgim nodded a shrug. "Kush-mai keeps his self to his self."

"Hoi, Gimgim," Ambarr said. He'd been in the back with his inventory, an oft-dusted collection of fasteners and hoo-dings and whatnots. In his hand he held the cover of an old hyper-drive, neutrino-ports dangling. "You got gallyblots today?"

Gimgim reached into the top of his cart and pulled out the sweet. "Just the one, Ambarr-mai?"

"Aah," Ambarr confirmed. "What's our Kush up to, then?" He indicated the shoe shop with one tendril, wrapped a second around the gollyblot, touched a third to the pay-screen on Gimgim's cart.

Now one Hupti exited Kush's shop, then another. They strode across the Via, horny feet clicking on the composite floor. Gimgim tilted so far to the side his vents nearly touched the floor.

"Move the cart, chai-chai," the first Hupti said. Then, to Ambarr: "You hight Ambarr Ping?"

"Ahh," Ambarr said. He'd already popped the gollyblot into his mouth. The word came out sticky and sweet.

"You will come with us." The Hupt officer indicated the direction Ambarr was expected to take with one sweep of his weapon.

There was a stunned silence. Then Cara said, "Hunh?"

"Ambarr Ping, you will come with us." There was a buzz in the Hupti's voice that said its vox-machine needed recalibrating.

"Whyever?" Ambarr said at last, swaying toward Cara and back again.

"You are compelled," the second Hupti said. At this, the last two officers came out of Kush's shop. Kush himself stood in the doorway, watching.

"Kush, you fool, what have you done?" Cara called to her brother. Then, "Go, Ambarr, I'll get to the bottom of this."

Ambarr handed the hyper-drive cover to his wife. "Well," he said, swallowing the gollyblot in one quick snap. The Hupti surrounded Ambarr, and marched him down the Via. Before they disappeared over the curve, Ambarr stretched one tendril up in confused farewell.

Gimgim straightened slowly, multiple eyes looking after Ambarr, and Kush, and Cara. Cara was already striding across the Via, even as Kush backed into his shop and slid the door shut.

"Kush!" Cara hollered, kicking the door. "You will tell me this instant what you have done!"

Kush elected not to. Cara continued banging at the door. Mingma and Ringma opened their door, theirs being the next shop spinward, to see what the commotion was about.

Mingma had obviously been aroused from sleep, it was rubbing its face and peering widely about. The dusty curtain hanging in the shop window on the other side of Kush's actually twitched. Of the methane breather next to Cara and Ambarr, there was, as usual, no sign.

"You come out this instant! Kush! The Hupti have taken Ambarr! What have you done?"

Ringma peered over Mingma's shoulder, then at the chai seller. Gimgim rolled his cart to the junk store, whispered the sad tale to Mingma and Ringma. Their mouths dropped open in dismay.

"Cara-mai," Mingma said, wrapping its robe around its shoulders and approaching. "Come in. We'll have chai and decide what to do next."

"Kush!" Cara screamed, kicking the door so hard that she dented it. "You will fix this, Kush!" Mingma draped one half of its robe over Cara, murmuring gently, drawing her away.

"I'll never speak to you again, Kush!" Cara cried. "You fix this NOW or I'll never speak to you again!"

Mingma steered Cara into its shop. Ringma helped Gimgim get the cart over the threshold. It clattered into the dusty silence and sat there, gleaming.

"Chai," Mingma said, settling the distraught Cara onto a stool. "Hothot, just like you like it." Gimgim pushed a cup into Cara's hands.

"I'll kill him, Mingma-mai," Cara said. "See if I don't!"

"Kill him after you've finished your chai," Mingma advised.

* * *

Kush had hoped to feel satisfied.

And he did, for a few heartbeats. The look on Ambarr's face! Priceless! He'd nearly choked on that damned gollyblot! Kush had wrapped himself in his tentacles and danced a one-two in his shop. Then Cara had crossed the Via, and Kush had felt his bubble of joy pop.

Cara was angry. Her skin had gone the dark shade Mother's used to when Kush had done something very bad. Her voice, saying his name, had made him want to change his name so it wasn't him she was screaming at. He hadn't been expecting that.

The voices of his neighbours' faded as their shop door closed. He could smell Gimgim's chai, spicey and sweet, and he salivated. He usually bought a cup at this time, but as Gimgim had gone into the junk shop with the others, it appeared Kush's chai would be late today.

Kush peered around his shop. He could still smell the oil of the Hupti weapons, the strange odour of their whirring and clicking parts. He could still see the impressions of their horny feet on his finefine carpet. One of them had knocked a display over. Kush used his fore-tendrils to straighten the display: bright boots for workdays and soft shoes for home-times. The store was quiet. It was always quiet at this end of the station, and with news going around that the Hupti had been here this morning, it would likely be even quieter than usual today. Kush considered taking the day off. Why not? He'd had a shock, hadn't he? Didn't he deserve a day off?

This thought brought back all the anger and all the hurt. Kush placed the last shoe carefully, then backed away, tendrils twitching with emotion. How dare he! How dare he even think about it! Kush felt a grim certainty settle on him. He was right to have called the Hupti. Ambarr deserved everything he got.

A soft chime sounded as the door opened.

"Kush-mai?"

It was Gimgim, the chai-seller. He had his cart with him.

"Good, Gim-mai!" Kush exclaimed, banishing his hurt feelings from his face. The honorific was a deliberate flattery. "I was just craving a cup of sweetspice! How timely!"

"I know my customers, Kush-mai," Gimgim said. Kush thought, however, that Gimgim's bow was slightly less deep than it had been yesterday and the sweetspice, when it was delivered, slightly less sweet than he liked. The suspicion took all the pleasure out of Kush's morning chai and he found himself wishing Gimgim would just go, rather than settling down on the bench, as he always did, for their morning chat.

But Gimgim was not inclined to leave.

Gimgim wanted to talk about Ambarr.

"I think, Kush-mai," Gimgim was saying, "that if you would go to the Hupt and tell them you were mistaken, they would release Ambarr-mai without delay."

"Why would I do that?" Kush sneered. "He is suspicious! Last week he spent two hours in the shop next door! With the curtains always drawn, who knows what goes on in there? Could be anything!"

"Malus-mai is a harmless old one," Gimgim soothed. Kush started. He had never heard the name of his neighbour, even after thirty cycles at the end of the Via on level 6. And Gimgim, who only passed through, knew not only the neighbour's name but also felt confident to judge if he was harmless or not!

"Ambarr has secrets in his soul," Kush said. "I know it, and soon the Hupti will know it."

"You know no such thing, Kush-mai," Gimgim chided. "You're small and angry and lonely, and it's your own fault. Ambarr loves you and would be your friend again if you could only set aside your foolfool pride. Cara-mai loves you, too, but if you don't fix this with the Hupt she'll never speak to you again. Nor will I, for that matter. You'll have to go all the way to level 4 for a decent cup of sweetspice."

"Ambarr deserves everything he gets," Kush said, but it rang a little less true than it had earlier.

Gimgim sighed. "This is my fault," he said.

Kush blinked. "What?"

"I thought I was being helpful, Kush-mai," Gimgim said. "I hoped that if you knew their plans you'd take the chance to fix things between you and Ambarr. I didn't expect you to do this."

"That has nothing to do with it," Kush insisted.

Gimgim stood. "You're a poor liar, Kush-mai," he said. "You need to sort this out, and quickquick, or you're going to turn into a lonely old man with curtains across your shop window." Gimgim opened the door, pushing his cart ahead of him.

Kush watched him walk down the Via, and then suddenly it was too much. He stepped out the door. "The sweetspice was not very good today!" he shouted after the chai seller. Across the Via, Cara saw him and slammed her door. The beads crackled and rattled.

Kush seethed. It was not his fault! He was innocent! Minding his own business (literally), and then there was Gimgim with his story and sad eyes and comforting pad on the dorsal hump. And 'maybe Kush-mai should talk to Cara and Ambarr,' and 'maybe Kush-mai should let by-gones be by-gones, before it's too late'.

"Cara!" Kush trumpeted, striding across the Via on long rear tendrils. Now it was his turn to pound on her door! The door opened. Cara stood there, ruff flaring.

"It had better be good, Kush," she said.

Kush spluttered. Kush found his words. "You should have

told me you were leaving!" he exclaimed. "I should not have found out from the chai seller!"

Cara's ruff drooped. "Was that was this was all about?" she asked. "You called the Hupti to take Ambarr away because of hurt feelings?"

"Well…" Kush said. "You should have told me."

"We wanted to tell you, you fool!" Cara snapped. "But you haven't spoken to either one of us in twenty-two cycles! Now suddenly you care about where we go and what we do?"

"I had to hear about it from Gimgim!" Kush protested. "How do you think that made me look?"

"Frankly, I don't care how it made you look," Cara snapped. "You don't have a say anymore in where we go and where we live. Ambarr has been nothing but a good and loyal friend, a kind and loving husband. And this is what you do?" She shook her head. "You've a smallsmall soul, Kush. Get your coat."

"What for?" Kush said.

Cara rapped him smartly with her dominant tendril. "To the Hupt section, fool, to get Ambarr released. And stop that waving. You're not in the right, Kush. You never have been."

***

By the time brother and sister arrived at the Hupt section, way way way at the top of level 2, Kush was much chagrined. Cara had wept all the time they passed through sections 5 to 3. The air was cool and thin in the upper sections, the light brightbright and the people…the people! Braxassia from Ttitxc on tall stilt-like legs; Mumeropi from Galapoood sucking on their pipes; round, silent Oofery from their nebula-orbitals. Many more Kush and Cara had never seen before, wearing a baffling array of colour and skin and clothes and scent. Cara shivered in her coat.

"You can't leave," Kush said. "You won't be happy out there." With his fore tendrils he indicated the black expanse of space beyond the composite walls of Fargone Station.

"We can't be happy here, either," Cara said. "No business, no future. We live off station shares, Kush, and they get smaller and smaller each day!"

"I don't need so much," Kush said, surprising himself with his generosity. "You could have some of mine!"

"We want a family, Kush," Cara said. "We'll never get a license as long as we stay on the station."

"You'll never break even on the shop. You'll probably never even find a buyer. And how could you afford the tickets?"

"We don't care about the shop. For a long time we thought we did. You remember the shop was Ambarr's aunts's, then his grandmother's before her? It was the granddam's legacy, Kush, but now the legacy is a weight keeping us from the life we want. We're leaving. We've been planning this a long, long time, Kush."

Truth was, citizens had been leaving Fargone Station for years. Since the Noaath conflict had really heated up, the colonies Fargone Station had been built to serve had gradually emptied. Fewer and fewer civilian ships came through. Then, for a while, it was all military heavy vehicles. That was a good time for business; Kush still kept a supply of military wear for when those ships came again. But that had been cycles ago, the war had moved further into the KriKriVi sector, and only the Hupti—who didn't need boots or shoes—had stayed behind.

The lift doors opened and they stepped out into section 2. It was silent except for the hum of life support. The silence was somehow more threatening than the mass of peoples on the lower levels. Cara hesitated. Where to now?

"Here," Kush said. He activated a terminal by the lift and

inquired after Ambarr Ping. There was a brief pause, and then lights along the wall lit up and pointed the way over the curvature of the floor and down a series of narrow corridors which ended in a small office with a desk. Behind the desk, a Hupti officer entered data into a 'screen.

Kush stumbled through an explanation.

"You filled out the proper forms," the Hupti said, checking its records.

Cara rapped Kush with her tendril. Confronting the Hupti officer, she'd gone uncharacteristically silent.

"Well," Kush stammered, "I made a mistake. Ambarr Ping is innocent."

"We have your signature," the officer stated. It's vox-machine rasped.

"I retract it," Kush declared.

"Please wait here," the officer said. Kush and Cara settled onto stools. The Hupt disappeared into a back corridor. The door swept shut behind it.

"Therethere," Kush told Cara. "They'll bring him out soon-soon and we'll all go home."

They waited.

They waited some more.

The Hupti officer came in again at one point and sat down. Kush rose on his tendrils. The Hupt said nothing. Kush sat down again.

When the Hupt left the room again, Kush said, again, "Soonsoon." But he didn't sound convinced.

Finally a monitor buzzed. Kush glanced around. Cara glanced around. The Hupt reentered the room and approached them. He handed them a scandisk.

"What's this?" Kush said, taking the disk.

"A copy of the charges levelled against Ambarr Ping at 3298, today," the Hupt officer said.

"The what?" Cara cried.

"But I didn't mean it!" Kush exclaimed. "I was just trying to scare him!" And, to give Kush credit, that sounded mean-spirited even to him.

"These are very serious charges, citizens." The Hupti read from his 'screen: "Conspiracy against a Governing Body, Forgery of Official Documents, Intent to Deceive a Governing Body, Disruption of the Peace, Smuggling with Intent to Deceive. The list goes on." The Hupt's vox-machine twitched and shifted to an approximation of empathy. "A lawyer is recommended. You may go."

There was a beep and a piece of memory paper slid out of a slot and onto the desk in front of them. Cara stared at. Kush picked it up. "What is it?" Cara whispered.

Kush read the card. "It's a preliminary hearing date," he said, nonplussed. "But it was a joke! A lesson, don't you see?" But the Hupti had turned its ears to 'off' and the lights were pointing, quite firmly, out of the office.

***

By the time Cara and Kush got back to level 6, blue section, Cara had had enough of Kush's excuses to last her another twenty years. They had made one stop on the way home: to a legal office on level 4 that had been recommended in a foot-note on the memory paper given them by the Hupti officer. Cara had left her contact information and kicked Kush in a hind knee when the secretary had required a deposit. Kush had touched the pay-screen reluctantly.

Now Gimgim, setting aside his regular schedule in favour of the upset in blue section, poured chai for all of them: Cara and Kush, Ringma and Mingma (whose pouch was humming from the busy mass of egglets nestled within), and himself. They settled into a cracked and faded conversation circle in front of the shuttered cinema.

"Yaya," Ringma said, settling back on its tail, "this smuggling business is very serious. Poorpoor Ambarr."

Fargone had closed its ports to war refugees ten cycle ago. The station, Command argued, no longer had the resources to feed and clothe and house the tens of thousands who were showing up at the docks on leaky barges day after day. Suffering from hypoxia, hyperthermia and various burns, lesions, broken bones and psychological trauma, the refugees were first placed in Fargone's vast, empty cargo bays. The intention had been to hold them there and then allow them to return home when the war abated. But as the war had been going on for millenia now, there seemed no hope of it ending. Then, the organisations which had promised help to the refugees had themselves succumbed to ongoing conflict. Fargone Station, telling its citizens that it, too, was a victim of war, had finally restricted its docks, even going so far as to fire on the unfortunate few who sought shelter here.

It was all politicking, of course. Fargone was the size of a small moon, and as many citizens were leaving the station as trying to enter. Had the refugees been given a place to call home and a chance to work, rather than locked idle into cargo bays, their numbers could have kept the station viable. But no, immigration was halted, Fargone, as a result, became closed to business, and its citizens packed their belongings and departed.

Refugees got in, of course, small numbers of them smuggled aboard cargo ships with sympathetic captains. They slipped into the populace with barely a ripple. Long-time citizens recognised them, if they cared to look: people with wide, nervous eyes who bore names that didn't quite fit their frames. They slid into spots left vacant by citizens who had moved on to better worlds and better lives, took up homes and businesses and identities which were not their own. For the most part, the diverse population of Fargone allowed them to blend in seamlessly.

"Freeloaders," Kush fumed. "Soon there'll be no real citizens left!"

"Shut it, Kush," Cara said. Then, to the others, "Why do the Hupti suspect our Ambarr? We mind our own business, keep ourselves to ourselves. Nothing happens down here! We've never even been censused!"

"Oh-oh-oh," Kush said suddenly. Mingma and Ringma exchanged looks. "What about the alarms going off in the middle of the night?" he said. "They went off again last night, did you hear them? Security never finds anything, but maybe there is something. Maybe."

"The security system is as old and falling-apart as the station, Kush-mai," Gimgim said, refilling Kush's cup.

"Mice and rats in the pipes," Mingma said.

"Cockroaches in the wiring," Ringma said. It sipped its chai.

"Nono," Kush said. "There's something going on, suresure. The station is full of Nuaath sympathisers. I read it on the newsfeed just last week." His voice dropped to a whisper. "They think the Bright is making too much money from the war, otherwise they would stop it."

"You give the Bright credit for control they do not have," Gimgim said quietly. "The Nooath Huupa are very powerful, and the insult done to them by the KriKriVi was great. The Bright has its hands full simply protecting Nooath's neighbouring systems."

"I don't understand why Fargone doesn't welcome incomers," Cara said. She looked around at the silent Via, the empty shops. "It would be so nice to see people here again! Remember how it was, Kush, when we were smallish?

Remember the vendors and hawkers? Remember the music and the dancers?"

"Ahh," Kush said, but he would not let the issue of smugglers and criminality go. "What about him?" he said, pointing at the methane-breather's shop, its windows filled with fog and an unidentifiable assortment of things on display. The airlock still held a curled 'going out of business' sign. It had been posted there as long as Kush could remember. "Why isn't he on the lower levels with the other methane breathers, ahh? Isn't that suspicious?" Kush swiveled on his stool, warming to his conspiracies. "Or that one, ahh?" He indicated the curtained shop with his dominant tendril. "Whoever sees him out and about? What goes on in there? That's the questions need asking, I tell you."

"He's a harmless old man," Ringma said firmly. "And that's the last we'll hear about our neighbours's from you, Kush-mai."

***

Cara reconsidered her feelings toward her brother, and decided she couldn't stand the sight of him, which was a hardship. Even though Kush had refused to speak to Cara and Ambarr for the last twenty-two years, Kush had relied upon, at least, catching Cara's eye now and then so he could reinforce that he wasn't speaking to her. Now, Cara was taking a mean kind of revenge on him. She never looked his way, never once, and when it was time to go speak to the lawyer, she took Mingma with her, not Kush. When it was time for the preliminary hearing, it was Gimgim who accompanied her, leaving his cart (the chai seller without his cart! How strange!) in the junk shop with Ringma and Mingma.

The day of the hearing, Kush busied himself with his inventory, shuffling dog-eared stock cards in hopes that something might have changed on them since the last time he'd looked.

Cara and Ambarr's shop was dark and shuttered. Kush disliked the look of that, as it reminded him of their plans to leave the station and start a family without him. The thought of it made him angry all over again, and the cold knot that had been twisting inside him since Gimgim had first shared the news grew a little tighter.

They wouldn't leave. They couldn't! They'd grown up here, knew no other life! They couldn't be happy anywhere else! Kush stopped his shuffling as a thought struck him. If he, Kush, uncovered the true smuggler (an easy task, he assured himself, criminal minds were not the sharpest), Cara and Ambarr would be so grateful they'd stay for sure! Kush might, might, mind you, consider renewing his friendship with Ambarr, if the other expressed his gratitude in a pretty enough fashion.

He occupied the rest of his day with planning, and was just about to put the first part of it in action when something strange happened. It was getting late, the lights dimming to reflect the circadian rhythm of species which had evolved planetside. Cara and Gimgim had not yet returned. Kush was pushing his footware display back into his shop. The door to the junk shop opened, and Ringma (or was it Mingma? The pair shared the burden of the eggsac between them and it was hard to tell which one it was) pushed Gimgim's chai cart out the door; being unaccustomed to the burden, the cart wobbled on the threshold. Before Mingma (or was it Ringma?) could right it, there was a muffled exclamation from inside the cart.

"Can I help you with that?" Kush asked.

Ringma (Kush recognised its voice as soon as it spoke) answered, "Thanks, no, Kush-mai, I have it," and lumbered off down the Via with the heavy cart.

When the lights in Cara and Ambarr's shop came on, Kush went straight over and knocked on the door.

"Ringma's up to something," Kush stated simply when Cara, after some hesitation, opened the door.

Cara looked tired. "Aren't you going to ask me about Ambarr?"

"Do you remember how quickquick Ringma was to explain the alarms away?" Kush said, excited. "Cockroaches in the wiring, he said! Cockroaches? In a space station? Ridiculous."

"What are you on about?"

"I saw Ringma with Gimgim's chai cart!" Kush exclaimed. "There was someone in it!"

"You've been watching those vids again, have you?"

"I heard the person cry out! Maybe Ringma's drugged him!"

Cara glared at her brother. "Will you call the Hupt on Ringma now? And then who? Mingma? Gimgim? Me?"

"If I tell the Hupt, then Ambarr will go free. Isn't that what you want?" Kush was confused. Was Cara's obsession with Ambarr's imprisonment clouding her mind?

"No...yes...oh, Kush, you foolfool creature!"

Kush waved his tendrils up and down, distraught.

"These are our friends, Kush. Our family!" Cara sighed. "Gimgim and Ringma and Mingma, the old man and the methane breather, even! Everyone else has gone, but we have stayed! I don't care what you think you know! Ringma is family!"

"But Ambarr..." Kush protested.

"You don't understand anything, do you, Kush?" Cara said, and closed the door.

***

It was a troubled Kush who went to sleep that night, and he was still troubled when the glitchy alarms woke him yet again. He lay on his pallet, watching the sulphur-yellow lights strobe across the shutters of his shop. Then he sat up. He had to know for sure.

Quietquiet, Kush shuffled to the door and peered through the shutters. It was full night in the Via, the emergency lighting throwing long, threatening shadows along the composite floor and up the walls. Other than that, it was still.

Then, a shape. Large and looming with a hunch-backed gait.

The methane breather, Kush thought, recognising the bulk of the respirator strapped to its back. Of course. He was tempted to call the Hupt right now, but he waited. Better to see what, exactly, the methane breather was up to.

It stopped outside Ringma and Mingma's. There was a fold in the darkness as the door opened. A figure darted out, followed by two, smaller ones, then a fourth. They were bipedal and slender, looking frail and delicate compared to Ringma (or was it Mingma?), who came out with them and shut the door behind it.

Then another figure! Gimgim with his cart!

Gimgim held the side of the cart open while the four creatures climbed inside. Then Gimgim and the methane breather strolled away down the Via casual as you please. Ringma (it might have been Mingma), adjusted the pouch with the eggsac and straightened. The alarm stopped. The lights went out. Kush was left in darkness, mind racing. He should call the Hupt. He'd seen the smuggling himself! He had proof! He could have Ambarr released and everything would go back to normal.

Or would it?

Cara didn't want to stay on Fargone. She wanted a family, and no birth licenses had been awarded on level six in fourteen cycles. However, so long as Ambarr was in lockdown, she wouldn't go anywhere. Maybe it was better that Ambarr stay where he was?

Kush had had more words with his sister in the last ten days than he'd had in the last twenty years. Even though most of the words were angry, they were, at least, speaking again. That was something.

Kush retreated to his pallet, considering. No one knew he'd seen anything tonight. No one need ever know.

***

No one told Kush that Ambarr had been released. The first he knew of it was when the party started, three days after the alarms had gone off.

Gimgim came by with his cart the next morning, his sideways bow of respect, Kush knew, signifying nothing. The chai seller poured the sweetspice, opening and closing the cart so efficiently that Kush—not for lack of trying—couldn't see within.

"Such good news about Ambarr-mai, ahh? Lack of evidence!" Gimgim said smilingly. "Why didn't we see you last night?

Kush had heard the music, of course, and the laughter. He'd sat inside, shutters closed, waiting for someone to come over and ask him to join them. He'd considered just going over to see what the get-together was about, but the longer he sat there, no one coming to collect him, the harder it had been to go out. By the time Kush realised no one would be coming, it was farfar too late to join the party. Everyone would know he'd been waiting for an invitation. His tendrils curled at the thought.

"I was busy," Kush said, and Gimgim accepted that excuse, though they both knew that the last time anyone had been busy on level 6 had been many, many cycles ago. Gimgim began to push his cart out of Kush's shop.

"Wait!" Kush said, and Gimgim did. Kush suddenly didn't know what he'd been going to say. There was an unpleasant tang in his mouth. Kush washed it down with sweetspice. "It's very good," he said.

"You're welcome, Kush-mai," Gimgim said. Halfway out the door, he turned back. "Kush-mai," he said, "you were missed, last night."

It was a kindness, but Kush knew the truth. He'd heard the music and the laughter, he'd seen his neighbours dancing on the Via.

He hadn't been missed at all, at all.

* * *

Cara came knocking the day before she and Ambarr were due to leave. Kush watched her cross the Via, and he retreated to the back of his shop, blood pounding in his ears. He felt his innards collapse to a small cold ball in his abdomen. Cara knocked.

"Kush!" she called. "I know you're in there! Let's not leave it like this!"

Kush, though he could not have said why, did not move.

"Kush! Brother!" Cara called again. "We're leaving tomorrow. Please, Kush, let's at least say goodbye to one another."

She waited outside his door. One minute. Three. Kush could see the shadow of her on the shutters. She remained still. Then, softly, "Kush?"

Kush's tendrils bent and he sank to a stool.

"Ambarr forgives you," Cara said. "I forgive you. We should have told you our plans. It was wrong that we didn't."

Her fore-tendril brushed the shutter. He could see her silhouette. "Please, Kush?"

Then,

"Our time-stamp is 7390, Kush. We'll be leaving at 62. Kush?"

Cara's shadow swayed over the shutters. She left.

***

Ambarr put the last bag by the door. The shop had been swept and dusted, the systems turned to 'low'. Cara had the keycard, minus the one she'd given to Gimgim, until he should need to pass them on.

"I'll just leave it on the counter, then," she said, putting the keycard down and arranging it neatly. It was worn, edges soft, older than Cara and Ambarr combined.

"I'm sure that's fine," Ambarr said. He barely looked at the keycard, which had once been his proudest possession. His two weeks in lockdown had hardened him somewhat. He'd come out looking taller, more grown into his shape. "Time to go."

The lighthauler they had reservations on had docked yesterday, the crew had switched out and now the ship was ready to depart. Cara and Ambarr would spend three months aboard, before transitioning to the deephauler which would carry them far from this outer system, counter-spinward, to a brand new superstation in the heart of the Bright. It had taken Cara and Ambarr eight cycles to save up the credit for the tickets.

"I should go to him," Cara said.

"You did."

"I should try again."

"Leave it, wife," Ambarr said gently. His tendrils wrapped hers. She leaned into him. "He's made his feelings clear." And so they stood, husband and wife, in the shop that had been home and shelter for them all their married life. "We should go," Ambarr said at last, clearing his throat.

Ambarr opened the door, took up their small cases. On the Via stood their neighbours: Ringma and Mingma (Mingma carrying, today, though the pouch did not look much bigger), the old man, leaning on his stick, even the methane breather, face obscured by the smoke from its respirator. Ambarr closed the door of the shop after Cara. Then, one by one, their neighbours swayed sideways (the old man's bow was stiff, but all the more touching for that). Cara felt emotion prick around her eyes.

"Good luck," Mingma said.

"Good voyage," Ringma added.

A glyph of friendship scrolled across the methane-breather's translator.

The geriatric bowed again.

Cara glanced toward Kush's shuttered shop. There was no sign of her brother. "I'll give him your message," Mingma reassured her. "I have it here," it touched a pocket in its overall. "He will get it."

"Many thanks, Mingma-mai," Cara said. Her voice was no stronger than a whisper.

"Here he comes!" Ambarr boomed. Cara's heart leapt, but it was the chai seller he'd seen, coming with his cart to help them carry their cases to the docking ring.

Gimgim stashed their bags in the cart, then it was time.

"We must go," Ambarr said, twining his fore-tendril around Cara's. They followed Gimgim, waving at their neighbours until the bend of the Via obscured them.

"Kush didn't come," Cara said.

"He has too much pride," Gimgim said. "He cannot bear to admit he is wrong."

"He is like our father was," Cara said.

"I remember your father," Gimgim said. "He had goodgood qualities, too."

"Thank you, Gimgim-mai," Cara said.

"Well spoken, Gimgim-mai," Ambarr added.

The lift from level 6 was empty save for the three of them. At level 4, some few others joined them. By the time they'd risen beyond command, the lift was half-full with citizens preparing to depart Fargone. No one spoke. They were long-timers, these people, Fargone citizens four and five generations past. Their ancestors had built the station, dreamed of a promising future for their children. None of them were leaving Fargone lightly.

Then the warning lights, and the computerised announcement. Cara draped a warm coat around herself. Ambarr did likewise. Gimgim did not, his species not bothered by the cold, or the heat. Pads and tendrils and grippers of various styles reached for safety-holds as the lift slowed and 'down' disappeared. The mag-clamps on Gimgim's cart engaged with a sharp click. The lift opened. Cold air rushed in, painful in the throat and the lungs. Cara gasped with surprise.

Scanners beeping, the citizens were directed this way and that. There was an interminable wait, then it was goodbye to Gimgim, whose all-level pass did not grant him access to the docking ring. Ambarr took the cases and grabbed hold of the C-dock rail. Cara said goodbye, took hold of the rail, and waited for the final door to open.

"Cara!"

It was Kush, shivering without a coat. He edged out of the adjacent lift shyly, a blush of uncertainty colouring him pink.

"Kush!" Cara dropped the rail, flung herself at her brother. Tendrils reaching, she embraced him like she'd not done since they were children.

* * *

"They asked me join them," Kush said, sipping his sweet-spice. It was hothot and delicious. Kush thought he might order another.

"Will you?" Gimgim asked.

Kush and Gimgim, Mingma and Ringma, were sitting on the bench outside Kush's shop. Kush paused, rubbed at the floor with a rear-tendril.

"It is a difficult decision," Mingma said. Its pouch hung comfortably from its abdomen, "but Fargone will always be your home, Kush-mai, whether you go, or not."

"And if you chose to go," Gimgim said, pausing, then continuing in a quiet rush, "you needn't worry about the shop. I can take care of it, like I took care of Cara and Ambarr." Gimgim offered another round of chai, on the house, while Kush considered what it was, exactly, Gimgim had done for Cara and Ambarr.

Kush watched Gimgim go. Mingma and Ringma sipped their chai. Maintenance must have done some work on the circulation system. The air smelled fresh and clean today. Kush felt he needed to fill the silence.

"So, when will they hatch?" he said, gesturing to the pouch.

Mingma and Ringma exchanged a look.

"Sorry, I didn't mean to pry!" Kush said quickly. But then something occurred to him. Cara and Ambarr couldn't get a license. No licenses had been awarded in fourteen cycles. How long was Mingma and Ringma's species' gestation?

Mingma leaned forward, spreading open the mouth of its pouch enough so Kush could glance inside. He had an impression of metal and wires, an interface, an antenna.

"We call it 'Cockroach'," Ringma said, laughing.

The glitchy alarms. Kush's eyes widened, then he felt himself blush. Not so 'glitchy' after all!

"Am I the only one not in on this secret?" he asked finally.

Mingma's tone was gentle. "Pretty much," it said, "although Cara-mai and Ambarr-mai knew nothing about it until Gimgim asked if they would let us have their shop."

"Their shop?"

"Those poor people have lost their homes, Kush-mai. They have nowhere else to go," Ringma said, "and Fargone needs citizens. Why shouldn't everyone benefit?"

"But…but what about the Hupt?"

"There is that," Ringma admitted. "After Ambarr was taken away we talked long and hard about what we were doing, how we were risking our neighbours. But, Kush, how can we see suffering, and do nothing?"

***

The next day, two bipeds moved into Cara and Ambarr's shop. They turned on the lights, turned the systems from low to high. Kush watched them from his bench, 'screen on his lap. He'd been reading the long history of the Noaath conflict. He'd learned much he had not known before.

Kush pushed himself upright, crossed the Via and knocked firmly on the door of the shop.

There was a long delay. The door opened. The biped's face was long and narrow, with wide, surprised-looking eyes and a deep slash of a mouth. Kush recoiled, wondering if the flap on either side of the head were some kind of overgrown gill.

"Can I help you?" the biped said.

Kush rumbled deep in his abdomen. The biped's accent was difficult to understand, its odour unfamiliar. "You should have the shop open by now," he said abruptly. "The Hupt don't usually come down here, but if they did, they would know the shop should be open by now."

There was a pause. "Thank you."

The biped was joined by a second, taller biped. It said something to the other in a language Kush did not know. The smaller one responded.

"Um," Kush said. "Um."

The bipeds waited patiently.

"You can ask me for advice," Kush said nervously, "if you need it." He jerked a tendril behind him. "That's me, over there. Shoes." He glanced down at their tiny, wedge-shaped feet. "It will take me some time to find shoes made for those," he said, "but I can do it."

"Thank you," the short biped said again after (presumably) translating for its partner.

Kush turned around. Then he turned back. "What do I call you?"

"I am Cara," the small one said. "And this is my husband, Ambarr Ping."

Kush managed a bow, deep and formal to hide a spasm of loss. When he straightened, his expression was open. Friendly, even, he hoped.

"Cara-mai," he said. "Ambarr-mai. I am Kush. Welcome to Fargone Station."

EARTH IS A CRASH LANDING

J.G. Formato

J.G. Formato is a writer and teacher currently living in North Florida with her beautiful family. Her short fiction has appeared in Syntax & Salt, Zetetic, Giants and Ogres: Fairy Tale Villains Reimagined, freeze frame fiction, and elsewhere.

I'm pretty sure I'm Trashcan Baby.

Star Baby would never spend her days in a cubicle processing gun permits for the great state of Florida. The requests are endless, the thanks are few, and the ramifications uncertain at best.

I wanted to see, though, if Star Baby was in there somewhere, underneath the skin. Dad said she was. The moon wasn't out, it was still new and a bit antisocial. But that's okay, it just meant I could see all the stars. And I'm not from the moon anyway.

I sank into the hammock, the nylon cords embossing my back with diamonds, and swung. Extreme stargazing, no blinks, always calms me down. I stared until the stars came alive, squirming against the restraints of darkness. My eyes watered and twitched, but I refused to lose my staring contest with the sky. By the time I was winning, the stars had joined me, dipping down and swimming in the resting tears.

One fell into the palm of my hand. Its glow crept through the periphery until it landed, squirming and tickling. Eyes on the skies, I closed my hand around it.

And crushed a lightning bug. The crunch was barely audible, yet utterly nauseating. Four of its six legs were bent at awkward angles, and I couldn't see the other two. Neon liquid, like a busted Halloween glow stick, smeared my palm and illuminated the horror. It was gross, and squishy, and dead.

Every sensory nerve in my body erupted, leaving my brain in the ashes of a personal Pompeii. I sprinted to the house and scrubbed my hands until they were red, then fell asleep with pillows on my ears, trying to drown out that tiny crunch.

***

It was horrifying and obligatory—the office birthday cake.

I knew it was coming. These were all folks that had watched way too many old sitcoms, the ones where everyone celebrates office birthdays with singing and cake. I thought it was just a TV thing, but shortly after I started working for The State, I found out it was a real-live human thing, too. And everybody thinks you're weird if you don't want to sing to people you don't know/like. Or be sung to by people you don't know/like. I should have called out this morning.

The horde of well-wishers poured into and around my cubicle, singing a mutilated version of the Happy Birthday song. It was like the one the staffy sings at Friday's, lots of clapping and chanting, but worse. They placed the cake before me triumphantly and my stomach turned. Unnatural blue blobs (flowers?) wreathed it, and I could pick out at least three distinct thumbprints. DNA evidence for days.

Gena, my cubicle neighbor, was smiling way too big, like she might hurt herself. It hurt my cheeks just looking at her. I was trying to figure out what she was so happy about when she pulled a shiny packet out from behind her back.

"Look, Celeste! Astronaut ice cream!" Her grin widened, and I got scared she was going bust that creepy vein in her temple.

"Oh, cool," I said, and did the expected chortle. I hated that I didn't know if she was's fucking with me or being sweet. Gena prides herself on being thoughtful, so maybe she was being nice, but it sure seemed like she was fucking with me.

"You know, like they eat in space." I didn't think she felt congratulated enough.

I was sorry I ever told her I studied astronomy in college. For one, it took me three months to convince her that I couldn't "do her horoscope." And two, every time I space out at team meetings she yells "Earth to Celeste!" and giggles until she turns red and snorts. It's not beautiful.

But mostly, I just hated to be reminded that I'm stuck here, bitter as hell, because I'm too scared to move away and actually get a job in my field.

Still, the astronaut ice cream seemed a much safer bet than fingerprint cake (vacuum sealed and all), so I nibbled a strawberry cube as the acquaintance mob spectated. The silence and eyes crushed me, until some jackass towards the back started the Happy Birthday abomination again. I needed to set the record straight.

"It's not really my birthday," I said. "It's just the day my dad found me. I don't have a birthday. So, you guys can just keep the cake."

The baffled stares reminded me that I probably am just Trashcan Baby. I should have just cut the stupid cake.

***

It wasn't until third grade that I found out I might be Trashcan Baby. The kids at school said I was. Actually what they really said was, "Trashcan Baby, stick your head in gravy!" I didn't stick my head in gravy, but I did go home and look it up on the internet. I have to admit, they had a case. The same year, month even, that I was born they found a baby in the trashcan behind McDonald's. They said it looked like the mom went into labor in the bathroom there (what must that have looked like?), and then chucked the baby girl in the trash on the way out. It was a big thing on the news.

I asked my dad about it, but he said it wasn't me. He said he wanted the Trashcan Baby and tried to adopt her, but they gave her to a nice Christian couple from Marianna. He was really sad about it.

But then he found me.

We were on the porch when he got home, my Star Mother and me. But he didn't see me at first. He was too worried about her. My Star Mother's body was sprawled out on the steps, twisted like a badly used Slinky. Silvery and metallic like a Slinky, too. Her fluid skin had a life of its own, though, rippling heavy clouds that swirled around her frame. Moonlight washed over her quicksilver flesh, and it shimmered in response. Her form was delicate, feminine, and broken. Dark mercurial liquid poured from the corners of her blackened mouth, and she stared up him with eyes that dripped galaxies.

That's what he said, anyway.

When she talked to him, her voice was in his head, and he heard her, not with his ears, but in the space behind and between his eyes. "Keep her safe, help her be human."

Dad knelt and took me from her long fingers. As he did, he felt my skin harden in his hands. The whirling mist of me stilled and became solid. He held me to his chest and my tiny heart began beating in time to his, slowing from its rapidly erratic rhythm. Mine followed his, and we knew we would love each other.

That's what he said, anyway.

He knelt by my Star Mother's side, cradling me between them. Tarry blackness gushed from her mouth and starry eyes, then she was gone.

Completely and forever. He felt a sudden and loving vibration, like a thunderclap, surge through the air as her body dematerialized. The air around us was thick and shiny, and I breathed in the sparkles that remained.

My body hardened more as weeks passed, and I grew a layer of human skin. But Dad said I kept the stars in my eyes, churning grey flecks in baby blue skies.

I may have grown a human skin, but I never felt comfortable in it. I made Dad tell me that story every night before bed. I couldn't go to sleep until I knew I was special. Not just "special."

I still tell it to myself as part of my bedtime ritual, but tonight it wasn't soothing. Since Dad died and left me, it was much harder to be an Earth Person. He used to explain everything so well, and there's nobody to do that now.

Maybe I should go back to being a Star Baby. Maybe she's still there underneath. Humaning's too hard.

I crept back down to the hammock and pulled off my pajamas. The ropes scraped against my bare skin, but I ignored the scratches, and hooked my toes into the cording and stretched my arms above my head. I bathed in the stars, letting the light penetrate my skin with trillion mile pinpricks. My body responded, tingling in the glow, ancient and familiar. It was lovely at first, tiny kisses covering my body, cooling my aggravated senses. It felt homey.

Then the sky kisses turned to teeth, and tore at my flesh with hungry mouths. The stars were devouring my earthly skin, ripping away the human shell. It was a labor of rebirth, painful and raw. Maybe even more so than actual birth, because you're doing it to yourself.

It was too much.

My skin undulated around me as I forced myself from the hammock and, tumbled into the rough grass. I dug my nails into the soil beneath the roots, a sensation that normally disgusts me, but I had to see if Earth would take me back.

She did. The tearing of my skin stopped, and I was safe in my cocoon of fake personhood. Thanks, Earth. I think. I don't know, it might have been a bit of a letdown. I wish I wasn't such a wimp.

I checked the mirror when I got inside, to see if I looked any different. Silvery freckles spattered my cheekbones. I couldn't tell if the stars had painted them on or rubbed some skin off.

Star Baby it is.

***

No one at work noticed my new glam face. After all, it wasn't my birthday anymore and they didn't have to sing for cake. They could pick at the congealed remains in the break room until they had completely consumed the last remaining crumbs of Celeste. I don't like it when people eat my name.

Not many permits were processed that day as I lurked about the cubicles, wanting people to notice my face, but not really notice. I wanted them to know I was special, but then again, that was my secret. I stared at them until they looked back, then ducked quickly behind my dark hair curtain. Don't look at me. I mean, look at me. Gah! Why are you looking at me?

It was a really long day. Eventually, I stopped eye-stalking my coworkers and sat down to Google solvents. Turpentine looked good. They had it at the hardware store and it seemed more "natural" than some of the other options. I made sure to get the "real" kind, the kind that's made out of trees. Fight Earth with Earth, you know. I was hoping to get stripped down, dissolve this layer of human skin, and find out who I was underneath.

You're supposed to be in a well-ventilated area when you use it, or you'll overdose on the overpowering pine-ness of it all or something, so I decided to use it in the backyard. I waited until it was dark and a few stars had popped out to keep an eye on me.

I rubbed it all over my skin with an old dishrag, until I smelled like a decayed, chemical forest, and climbed into the hammock. My skin prickled all over as more stars broke through the night sky. It burned a little bit. I should have gotten one of those big silver tanning reflector things, the kind ladies always use in old movies when they're sunbathing.

Maybe the backyard wasn't ventilated enough, because I passed out beneath the weight of the sky and smells. And when I woke up, I wasn't sure I woke up. I felt squishy, like a water balloon. I kind of looked like a water balloon, too. My skin was thin and translucent. Beneath its wobbling surface a wet fog scintillated, sparkling as it swirled around my core of bones.

Walking felt like floating, and I splashed inside my feet. The last spidery web of human skin clung to my Star Self. Just a little more off the top.

The can of turpentine was on the porch, and I made my way slowly over. I couldn't actually feel my muscles, I just directed my hazy innards. It took a long time.

I sat on the steps, where my mother had left me, and rubbed the dampened cloth over my legs. I wondered if I looked like her, inside.

And then I saw her. She slithered along the grass, a floating mist in feminine form creeping over the green blades.

"Mother?" The word plunged from my mouth, rushing like a waterfall.

She reached the bottom step, her damp curling fingers clinging to the splintered wood. Black eyes, dimmed clouded nebulas, stared up at me. She shook her head slightly, which must literally be the universal symbol for No.

"I knew her, though," she said. Not out loud, but in the space between my eyes and nose. A vibration that emanated from my sinus. "You look like her. Underneath. I knew it was you when I set the course. Your glow called to me across space and time."

She pulled herself up on the step next to me, and I saw the black liquid dripping from her mouth and ears. "You're hurt."

She nodded, then smiled. "Earth is a crash landing. It takes a lot of personal momentum to make it here. I don't mind. I got her here safely." She ran her hand up her chest and pulled from her ribs an infant, perfectly formed and rippling like Mercury. "You'll take care of her, I know. Teach her to be human. It's safer here. Home is not a good place for our girls."

"No?" I was surprised. I've always thought I'd fit in there. That it was Earth that was all wrong.

"Our girls are slaves." An icy blue mist emanateds from her eyes. Tears.

"You?"

"Me. Your mother. But not you. Not her," she said as she placed her little one in my hands. "We got you out. You have a chance here."

The Star Baby grabbed my pinky and laughed, a sweet thrumming that washed over my sinus cavity. Her rapidly churning skin stilled and hardened in my grasp and, my fading and lucent skin hardened in hers. The vibration came next, the loving supernova that signals a Star Mother's last sacrifice. Salty Earth-water tears flowed from my eyes—there were so many more things I wanted to ask and say. Instead, I breathed the sparkles that hung in the air.

I looked down at the wriggling little mass in my arms, my Star Baby. Her eyes were twin galaxies, and I named her Andromeda on the spot. I can call her Andy for short. That's cute.

Nestled against my chest, she cooed musically in time to my heartbeat, and we knew that we would love each other. We'll figure this Earth thing out together. I'll never be a traditional human, but now I have enough personal momentum to make it here.

THANK YOU

Many thanks to our patrons
and supporters, especially:

Natalie Weizenbaum

Cathrin Hagey

Tory Hoke

GriffinFire

Want to see your name here? Become a patron!

patreon.com/lunastation

ABOUT THE COVER ARTIST

Sara Kipin is currently a senior illustration major attending the Maryland Institute College of Art in Baltimore. As a child, she was gifted many illustrated fantasy books from her family and has now taken that inspiration with her into her adult years. Once graduated, she hopes to use these aesthetics as a book illustrator or a preproduction artist.

Learn more about Sara and see her work at:

http://sarakipin.tumblr.com

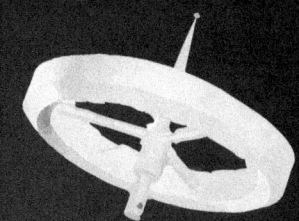